"You don't play fair."

"No," Vigadó agreed softly. "I never do. Because I always have to win."

And he kissed her.

For a moment Mariann clung to his warmth and then pushed away, her eyes dark with confusion. "You're an accomplished lover, I'm sure," she said unsteadily. "But sex and lust have nothing to do with hearts and souls."

"So spend the night with me and teach me all about love," Vigadó challenged mockingly.

DESTINY awaits us all, and for Tanya, Mariann and Suzanne Evans—all roads lead east to the mysteries of Hungary.

Tangled Destinies

As Tanya arrives in Hungary for her younger brother's wedding, her older brother, István, lies in wait after four years. He's the only man she's ever loved—and he's hurt her. But what he has to tell her will change the course of her life forever.

Unchained Destinies

Editor Mariann Evans is on a publishing mission in Budapest. But instead of duping rival publisher Vigadó Gábor, she is destined to fall into his arms.

Threads of Destiny

Suzanne Evans' attendance at the double wedding of her sister Tanya and her brother, John, presents a fateful meeting with mysterious gate-crasher Láslό Huszár. He's the true heir to a family fortune and he has a young family of his own. He is about to make sure that his complex family history is inextricably linked with hers, as all the elements of this compelling trilogy are woven together.

A Note to the Reader:

This novel is the second part of a trilogy. Each novel is independent and can be read on its own. It is the author's suggestion, however, that they be read in the order written.

SARA WOOD

Unchained Destinies

DESTINY
BOOK
2

Harlequin Books

TORONTO • NEW YORK • LONDON
AMSTERDAM • PARIS • SYDNEY • HAMBURG
STOCKHOLM • ATHENS • TOKYO • MILAN
MADRID • WARSAW • BUDAPEST • AUCKLAND

ISBN 0-373-11796-5

UNCHAINED DESTINIES

First North American Publication 1996.

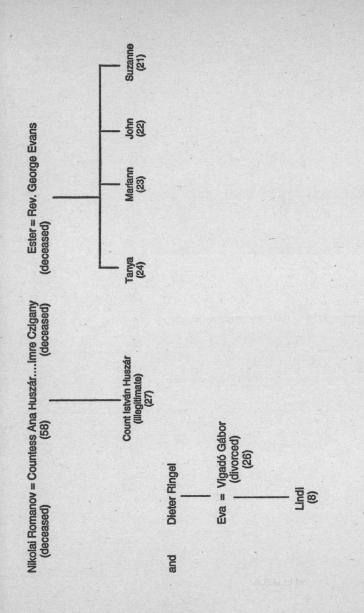

Nikolai Romanov = Countess Ana Huszár.....Imre Czigany
(deceased)   (58)   (deceased)

Ester = Rev. George Evans
(deceased)

Tanya   Mariann   John   Suzanne
(24)   (23)   (22)   (21)

Count István Huszár
(illegitimate)
(27)

and   Dieter Ringel

Eva = Vigadó Gábor
(divorced) (26)

Lindi
(8)

CHAPTER ONE

'BULLSEYE!'

Mariann paused in the doorway of her new boss's office, taken aback by his cry of triumph. Oh, good! she thought. He's a bit zany! She saw he'd been playing darts—a healthy sign, she reckoned, in a man she'd judged to be under stress.

But when he turned there was a startling malevolence in his expression and she took the dart he thrust towards her with a wary concern. Ordinary bosses were difficult enough; she wasn't too keen to play games with a maniacal one! What *was* his hang-up?

'I'll pass on the darts,' she said pleasantly. 'I came to——'

'Throw it,' he growled, jerking his head at the wall opposite.

Her sister Tanya had always said publishers were mad! Mariann stifled a giggle and balanced the dart between finger and thumb to humour him, turning her attention to the large photograph which had been skewered to the noticeboard by three other darts.

For a moment her hand wavered. Staring back at her was a man who seemed to burn holes in her. 'At him? Who is he?' she murmured in awe.

'You *must* know Vigadó Gabór!'

Now she understood! Like many other publishers, Lionel had suffered because of this man. For several seconds, Vigadó's intense animal quality held her quite still. It was the eyes that mesmerised her, glowering out black and full of malevolence from under lowered brows, capturing her, drawing her to him as surely as if she were being tugged on a rope like a slave!

'Extraordinary guy!' she managed, quite unreasonably disturbed. How infuriating! Her self-respect, her female pride was ruffled. Men *never* had that effect on her.

'You said it.' Lionel sounded strangely pleased.

'Where's his nice toothy smile for the photographer?' she asked wryly, and studied the rest of him. Wide shoulders. An expensively toned torso beneath that expensively tailored navy suit. Dark as the devil. And a scar that slashed into an inch or so of his Slavonic cheekbones, lending him a disquieteningly exciting air of wickedness. 'Wow! How did he get that?' she murmured.

'Duelling, they say.' Her boss seemed to be watching her reaction like a hawk.

She laughed in disbelief. Too romantic! 'Oh, yes?'

'He's a wild, impetuous Hungarian with a vile temper——'

'Fighting over a woman?' she hazarded, seeing the possibility instantly.

'*Women*,' answered Lionel scathingly.

She wasn't surprised. He had a mouth to make bones liquefy and a jaw... She smiled. That jaw told everything: his ruthlessness, the tenacity, the way he'd swept through the publishing world like a scourge. He'd been the talk of the Frankfurt Book Fair.

Her dart flew arrow-straight and lodged between a pair of wickedly sculptured lips. 'Will that do?' she said, giving a small laugh to clear the effect of Vigadó's dynamic eroticism on her.

'Till you skewer him in person,' said Lionel bitterly.

'I'm your new editor, not your hit-man,' she grinned.

Entirely against her will, she found herself looking at the photograph again. Two-dimensional or not, Vigadó looked ready to leap out from his glossy paper prison at any moment and tear his many enemies apart with his teeth.

'I think it's time someone made a stand against him.' Lionel slumped in his chair. 'He's devoured half the publishers in Europe. What do you know of him?'

Mariann considered. 'Gossip, mostly. I know he's a street-fighter and not a gentleman by any means. He head-hunts authors. He's taken some of yours—and he has an agent in Hungary, like you.'

'He's trying to ruin me,' said Lionel quietly.

Her sympathetic eyes noted the despair in every line of his body even while her own apprehension made her heart beat faster. This was her first editing job. Her first step on the ladder. If Lionel went under, so would she. More interviews. More lecherous bosses. She sighed.

'He can't want a small publishing house,' she began.

'It's a matter of vindictiveness!' Lionel raised a face consumed with hatred. 'I could kill him! He's threatening the existence of this precious company I've built up from nothing—*nothing*!'

'You still have Mary O'Brien,' Mariann soothed hastily.

'Not any more!'

'*What*?' she cried in dismay.

Her boss poured out a large whisky and Mariann realised with concern that it was about to follow the route of several others. 'Last week I went to Cork,' grated Lionel, 'to discuss the editing of Mary's final six chapters. She'd vanished—gone into hiding, God knows where. Her letter said it all. Vigadó's poached her!'

'That's unethical! Outrageous!' gasped Mariann. 'Mary's your best-selling author——'

'And without her I'm finished,' her boss said grimly, hurling the last dart wildly at Vigadó's merciless face.

'Why?' asked Mariann, appalled.

'Let me spell it out for you. The bank knows Mary's done a bunk. That swine must have told them. They're reluctant to continue my overdraft and I can kiss goodbye to any hope of venture capital loans. This business *eats* money! I might as well slit my throat and be done with it!' he yelled.

And he looked as though he might, given any more blows to his professional pride. 'You can't throw in the towel! Don't let him win!' she cried hotly. 'I'll stand by you, I'll do anything I can.' Her voice softened with sympathy and became coaxing. 'OK, Vigadó's stolen your authors—so what? He doesn't have the one thing that made this company successful: *you*. If you built up your publishing house before, you can do so again.'

Lionel gave a mirthless laugh, looking more haggard than ever. 'You don't understand! I need Mary,' he insisted. 'She's one blockbuster author that even the banks have heard of. She guaranteed our loan merely by being on our list. Mary can make a fortune for us. We nursed her, encouraged her, saw her through all her crises and published her first book, then the rest...'

'What about her contract?' said Mariann quickly. 'She must be in breach of it. We can——'

'No.' He shook his head. 'She was in between contracts. We'd been ... discussing fresh terms.'

Mariann groaned. 'What awful luck! But ... perhaps one of those manuscripts on my desk will turn up another Mary——'

'You know the odds!' he said, impatiently dismissive. 'I can't afford to wait for the unlikely. Mariann, you're my only hope!'

'Me? I'll read till the words blur for you, but I've been an editor's secretary for the last two years. You only interviewed me for this job a few days ago! I'm not exactly your most experienced member of staff!' she protested.

'You're the most beautiful, though.' He clamped a sweating hand on hers, his expression that of a desperate man.

Her mind whirled uncomprehendingly and she drew back, her eyes narrowed. 'What did you say?' she asked coldly.

'I have a job for you. A very important one. Get Mary back.'

She blinked, not seeing the connection. 'How——?'

'You speak a little Hungarian. You've not long come back from Hungary.' He looked at her for confirmation.

'Yes. I went for my brother's wedding. John works there,' she said, frowning—and omitting to say that the wedding never took place. 'My sister Tanya is marrying a Hungarian—István Huszár.'

Suddenly she picked up his drift. Vigadó worked for Dieter Ringel, the vast, international publishing house. He'd risen sky-high in that organisation via his wife's bed, marrying Dieter Ringel's only daughter. But Vigadó was Hungarian by birth.

She slid her hand away. 'I suppose you've heard somewhere that István is a pretty influential guy,' she said slowly. 'I want to help, but I won't use him to——'

'It's your own talents I want!' broke in Lionel. 'Vigadó's moving the fiction department of Dieter Ringel from London to Hungary. That means the records will be on their way to Budapest. Mary O'Brien's hideaway address will be in his office files. Charm your way into the office. Make tea, service the drains, anything! My agent will give you every assistance. He knows his job is at stake too. When you're alone, search for that address. Mary has always liked the intimacy of our small company and scorned conglomerates. If I can get to her, I can persuade her to return, I'm sure.'

Drains? He was raving! 'Everyone knows that Vigadó works all night like a vampire,' she pointed out. 'Even if I did gain access, I'd never be alone long enough——'

'The *Bookseller* says he's not leaving London himself till the end of the month. That gives you three weeks.'

'Good grief! You're serious! Commercial espionage!' Gracefully she lowered herself into a deep chair and looked at him in amazement from under her thick, dark brows. 'Lionel, the chances of my getting work in his office is nil——'

'Don't you look in a mirror?' he snapped irritably. 'God, Mariann, they'll take you on just so they can look at you! You'd tempt a whole monastic order!'

Putting his exaggeration down to stress, she flicked a glance down the neatly waisted scarlet jacket and brief coral skirt. 'I look good,' she acknowledged. 'I get eyed up, but——'

'No. Not *good*. That's the point. Oh, I'm sure you say no more often than most women brush their teeth, but that's not the impression you give out,' said Lionel impatiently. 'I don't know what's in your background, but it sure isn't goodness! You've got legs a man could dream about, wondering where they ever end, a mind-boggling body that sways with invitation whenever it moves and eyes that would lure an ice-man to his fate!'

Her mouth gaped open. He'd given no hint of the way he saw her. She'd virtually taken the job because he seemed preoccupied with other concerns and not the length of her legs.

'Lionel!' she said sharply, stiffly. 'This is my second day. I'll make it my last if——'

'Oh, god!' he groaned, burying his head in his hands. 'You don't know what I'm going through. He's sleeping with my wife!'

Mariann's eyes widened. No wonder Lionel was at his wits' end and suggesting this hare-brained scheme! A believer in constancy where marriage was concerned, she glared indignantly at the photograph. Vigadó was evil—and looked it. A modern-day pirate, burning and sinking companies, press-ganging the crew and taking hostages. Poor Lionel, to be up against that monster!

'I'm so sorry,' she said gently.

'Adding insult to injury,' muttered Lionel, 'he's given my wife a job as senior editor!'

She gasped, pained by such a cruel betrayal, and thought how good it would feel to pay Vigadó back for his double-dealing. Crazy! Or was it? Her head lifted high on its long, honey-skinned neck, a reckless smile curving the lush lips with their permanently uptilted corners. Supposing she succeeded? What a coup! Ideas piled into her head.

Hi! I'm your local, friendly plumber... I'm checking your telephones ... Rat-infestation inspector here...

Amused by her inventiveness, she glanced at the malefic Vigadó, felt a jolt of raw sexuality and resented him for producing it. He was ripe for his come-uppance. And perhaps she could deliver it by helping Lionel to steal back his brilliant author.

It was a terrific gamble—but rather exciting! And if it came off, her job would be secure. Her dream profession would be solid reality. Even if she were caught searching the files, she could find some excuse like... What am I doing? Why, I've lost one of my eyelashes! she imagined herself saying, with a blandly innocent smile. Mariann's bold sense of the dramatic leapt with the prospect of a full-blown, real-life part to play.

And she'd see her dear sister Tanya, István, John, *and* the fizzing, exotic city of Budapest again... She grinned, conveniently sweeping obstacles away and dreaming of gorgeous pastries, the magic of the snow, the passionate arguments with husky-accented Hungarians over Turkish coffee...

'OK,' she said impulsively, her eyes glistening with anticipated pleasure. 'The sticky buns clinched it. I'll give it a go—and we'll beat the brute at his own game!'

'Oh, bless you, bless you!' breathed Lionel triumphantly.

Involuntarily, she slanted her sloe eyes to the watchful Vigadó. His gimlet stare was directed straight at her in challenge. 'Viggy, sweetie,' she murmured, hoping to cheer Lionel up, 'are you in for *trouble*!'

'Oh, a-dabbin' it here, a-dabbin' it there, a-sloshing it- Whoops!' Feeling immensely exuberant now her fellow decorators and the staff of Vigadó's Budapest office had gone home and she was alone, Mariann halted her raucous song in mid-roller stroke. 'Drop the "g",' she reminded herself with a giggle. 'Keep in character!'

A dollop of paint dropped on to her bare shoulder and she remembered that she'd been tempted to leave Vigadó's office reeling from a rash of purple spots, but had overcome the urge!

Her peal of infectious laughter echoed around the empty room as she sidled barefoot along the plank between two ladders. 'A-sloshin' it here and a-sploshin' it there...'

She'd done enough. Operation Search, begin! she thought, and a thousand butterflies suddenly took flight inside her stomach. That was natural, she grimaced.

She'd never done anything criminal before. So far, she'd only skirted the fringes of deception. Now she was breaking and entering. It was still a lark—and she hoped it would remain so. Lionel had seemed thrilled at her clever deception, eagerly demanding to know every detail of her plan.

Carefully she flicked some paint over herself in a few strategic places in case the janitor came in and clambered down. Everything had gone so well! Lionel's agent had come up trumps. Impersonating Vigadó, he'd ordered two decorators to start work on the offices immediately—and to take on Mariann to help them. Here, the agent had made his voice husky with a few dropped hints.

'I'm sending her to Budapest ahead of my arrival, giving her a job, somewhere to stay and . . . well, I hope she'll show her gratitude,' he'd purred.

Glad of the highly priced job, the decorators hadn't seen through the deception and had willingly agreed. Why should they care who she was? They had work.

They'd swept in that morning, full of confidence, and no one in the panic-filled building had dared to question 'Vigadó's' arrangement. The staff were too taken up with organising order out of chaos, ready for Vigadó's arrival—and the manager was more than busy grumbling that he was having to give up his beautiful, spacious office to his boss. She and the decorators had shifted out the antique furniture and spent the rest of the day rubbing down the paintwork and washing the walls while she'd simpered and wriggled seductively out of her boiler suit to lend credibility to her story by displaying a few assets.

Whenever possible, she'd made it clear to anyone who'd listen that Vigadó had picked her off the streets and she was immensely grateful. And when she'd prettily begged to start the ceiling that evening so she could ring Vigadó later and tell him how well she'd done, no one had liked to refuse. The Great Man obviously terrified them all!

Cowards! Her eyes gleamed. In the adjoining office, and now facing her, was the manager's desk—and the keys to the filing cabinets. She'd particularly asked him to lock them up before they were moved out and had seen where he'd put the keys.

Stealthily she took the keys, slid the small one into the lock and heaved out the 'B' drawer... Nothing there about Mary! And before she had time to push the drawer shut and try the 'O's, she heard a sound outside and was forced to scamper back up the ladder and on to the board again. Shaking with nerves, she ran the roller up and down the tray, picking up a load of flapjack-coloured paint.

"Oh,' she belted out noisily, 'a-dabbin' it here, a dabbin' it there——!'

'A beautiful intruder, I do declare,' came a dry male drawl.

'Wooahhh!' yelled the startled Mariann, seeing who it was and wobbling perilously as a result, her whole body lurching about from the shock. Vigadó! she thought wildly. Why? How——?

'Watch the——!'

'Oh, lor'!' she wailed. Paint sloshed out from the shallow tray and hurled flapjack stains all over her shorts but with the dreaded Vigadó around she knew her priority: the ridiculous Marilyn Monroe wig that Lionel had proudly chosen and insisted she wore.

'Hold on!' rapped the harsh voice.

'I—*am*!' she grated irritably. Darn him! Why was he here? He was ten days early! The dart-riddled face in the photograph flashed before her eyes. The glacial stare. The menacing expression... 'Ohhh! Help!' she cried, teetering precariously as her uneven weight tilted one of the ladders.

She heard his luggage hit the floor and the sound of his quick strides heading towards her. But her centre of gravity had given up the unequal struggle and, with both hands jammed on the wig, she toppled helplessly towards Vigadó Gabór's waiting arms.

He caught her with effortless ease, as though he prac-
tised twice a night—which he probably did, she decided
angrily, since he'd turned her around deftly and slid her
to the ground to face him with the skill of a man ac-
customed to arranging scantily clad women where and
how he pleased. She blushed at the carnal images she'd
conjured up.

'Stupid female!' he growled, pushing her away. She
almost crumpled to the floor on infuriatingly boneless
legs so he caught her again, reluctantly folding her limp
and shaking body to his rock-like chest, his open coat
snuggling around her of its own accord. 'Why the hell
did you grab your *hair*?' he added, with irritatingly *mas-
culine* exasperation.

She grinned. Because it would have fallen off
otherwise! With her face pressed hard into his vicuña-
coated shoulder, she searched her frantically spinning
mind for an explanation.

'I paid a fortune havin' it done,' she gasped breathily,
saying the first thing that came into her head.

'God! Women!' he grunted contemptuously and she
sensed that he'd raised his eyes to her flapjack ceiling.

But he did pat her back soothingly so she obliged him
and his prejudices with a trembly, ultra-feminine sniff.
Lionel had told her on the phone to seem innocent, ignorant, a tart with a heart. Initially she'd protested, intending to play it straight—and only slightly over the
top. Then she'd listened to Vigadó's staff talking and
her qualms about deceiving them had vanished. They
were so proud of their boss's ruthless, piratical tactics
that she'd decided they were equally guilty of unfair
business practices.

And now, unexpectedly faced with the dangerous viper
himself, dumb stupidity might be a wise move!

'My heart's goin' nineteen to the dozen!' she breathed,
waiting to see how he was going to react. Like a healthy
male, she hoped, diverted by a pretty face.

'So it is. Kind of you to draw my attention to the
throb in your breast,' he said mockingly, his Hungarian
accent enhanced by the deep and husky timbre.

Mariann blushed at his directness. 'I meant——'

'Your acrobatics were dangerous. You could have broken your neck. How very foolish.'

She suppressed a smile of triumph. It was obvious he thought she was a dense, fluffy-headed female, and she wasn't going to disillusion him! Fluffiness suited her in the circumstances; he'd never suspect her of any greater crime. And . . . it would be amusing to pull the wool over the eyes of such a womaniser, for Lionel's sake . . .

'Oh, my! I never thought of that!' she cried in simulated horror, her voice muffled by his shoulder. 'You've got to admit, though, if I'd ended up as dead as frozen chicken in a freezer, my hair would have looked nice,' she reasoned idiotically, dying to laugh out loud and share the joke with someone.

His chest heaved up and down at her logic and Mariann realised to her amazement that he was trying not to laugh too. A monster with a sense of humour? she marvelled.

'Can't argue with that,' he said evenly. 'Now who . . . ?'

He paused and went quite still for several seconds while the hairs on Mariann's neck lifted in sheer apprehension. He was facing the other office. Could he see the open cabinet from there? She began to shake.

'Somethin' wrong?' she croaked, feeling the quick rise and fall of his broad chest. And she also sensed an increased alertness; he was suddenly on guard. Surreptitiously she tried to check the wig.

'Yes,' he answered softly and Mariann tensed. 'There's paint on your hair.' She breathed again. Paint! And she'd been afraid that he'd been putting two and two together, had looked right inside her head and read the words 'Commercial Spy' written there! 'Looks like a repeat visit to the hairdresser,' he mused, trying to lift one of her hands which was still locked rigid on her scalp.

'Don't!' she said hastily, afraid he'd pull the wig askew. 'I don't like it being mussed up. The paint'll wash out,' she added, lifting her face from the shelter of his expensively soft coat and pushing herself back a little. Thinking she'd been a bit abrupt, she gave him a 'my hero' smile. 'Thanks for catching me,' she said politely, and met his gaze properly for the first time.

Wow! she thought in stunned admiration. What ruinously liquid eyes! Melting chocolate, she mused, and then recoiled in alarm because the chocolate seemed to be darkening and thickening as though he found her attractive. He shouldn't have eyes you could dream in! she thought crossly. He should be cold and vicious with an icicle gaze, jagged teeth and foul breath!

Lionel had shown her articles and told her tales about this man to make her stomach turn. Staff meetings in rooms without chairs so no one waffled. High pay, long hours, ruthless sackings. Phone-tapping and bugging of his competitors' offices and a no-hands-barred policy of seducing any woman who might aid his head-hunting expeditions. Secretaries in hysterics. Desperate husbands, suicidal wives whom Vigadó had loved and left.

A man with no morals. Furthermore, a man with only one aim: a driving need that amounted to an obsession to dominate everyone he came across, reducing strong men to quivering wrecks, tough editors to tears, boardrooms into submission.

He was certainly intent, she noticed angrily, on making the most of having a blonde fall like manna from the skies! In panic, she fought down a rush of sinful sensation as his mouth almost nuzzled her cheek. Her hands pushed the broad shoulders but she was locked in place by his immovable arms and all that happened was that her spine arched back and she was staring at his mocking lips.

'I had no choice but to catch you,' said his lover-close mouth, letting the lover-husky voice wash warm breath over her dizzily sensitised skin. 'I walked in, saw a pair of provocative bare legs waving around at eye-level, and then a beautiful blonde fell into my arms. And she began to tremble appealingly, virtually asking for...I wonder what?'

Mariann stiffened. He'd changed from showing anger at the intrusion to acting like a hunter who'd found his dinner wandering provocatively around his lair. That was a deliberate opening gambit—but how to handle it? she wondered. Should it be the usual joky, gentle let-down, or a quick nipping in the bud? Infuriatingly, she couldn't risk annoying him!

'I had a shock,' she confided. 'Me past life zipped past me eyes.'

'Oh! That must have been a dreadful experience to go through. I sympathise,' he murmured insincerely.

'Ta. I'm okey-dokey now,' she assured him. 'Give a girl a bit of breathin' space, there's a duck!'

'No,' he said succinctly.

Mariann was taken aback. 'No?' she repeated.

'I'm hanging on to you till we establish what you're *doing* in here,' he said in a brittle voice, his grip tightening. 'These are *my* premises and it's after office hours, even Hungarian ones.'

'I know,' she said as cheerfully as she could, comparing him mentally to his photograph. He looked much more dangerous in the flesh, as if he'd flick their darts back and deliberately pierce a few of her vital arteries. Darn it, she'd have to soften him up and lull his suspicions by being moronic! And bluff like mad. 'You're the home-grown whiz-kid!' she said with girly admiration.

'I reckon I am,' he agreed, his cynical gaze resting thoughtfully on her. 'Vigadó Gabór. And you?'

'Mimi,' she supplied and flashed a witless smile, deeply disappointed that she dare not risk saying, Call me Mimi!

'Mimi,' he repeated and his eyes narrowed suspiciously.

Mariann didn't blame him. It had seemed a harmless and appropriate choice when she'd been confronted by Vigadó's lecherous office manager. Being 'Mimi' had made her feel coy and less inclined to ruin everything by crushing him with well-directed scorn when he'd suggested bringing a bottle of wine around to wherever she was staying.

Now, with this worldly-wise, laser-sharp tycoon dwelling on the likelihood of the name—instead of being mesmerised like the office manager by the way her vital statistics moved—she sensed she'd made a mistake.

So she grimaced and shrugged. 'Daft name, ain't it?' she chirruped.

'Yes. Very.' To her dismay, Mariann's body betrayed her, tightening with apprehension at his increasingly cynical glance. 'You're extremely tense. Women usually relax in my arms. Are you afraid of me?' he asked with apparent innocence. But his voice had a steely edge to it.

'You've got such . . . extraordinary eyes!' she admitted huskily. 'All glinty, like butcher's knives. Give me the shivers, they do!'

'My eyes are telling you what I'm thinking,' he said tightly. 'You see, I don't take kindly to intruders, Mimi.'

'Intruder?' She bristled. 'I'm legit!'

'Legit what?' he drawled.

Her head jerked confidently in the direction of the ladders. 'Decorator, of course! Have paint tin and sandpaper, will travel!'

'Really. Then why the nerves?'

Annoyed with herself, she tried to ease her tension and widened her eyes in simulated awe. 'Dunno. But I've never been this close to a millionaire before!'

'Billionaire,' he corrected, reaching out unexpectedly to smooth her hair back off her face.

'Ooh! Don't! Tickles!' she gurgled in panic, arching away. He'd find the join!

His mouth thinned. He was quite unaffected by her girly appeal, she realised in dismay. 'How did you know who I was when I first walked into the office, Mimi?' he asked with a sudden, devastating softness.

For a fraction of a second, she didn't know what to say, then managed to pull herself together. 'I'm not *daft*!' she replied scornfully. 'Who else would have a key?'

'The janitor.'

'In a vicuña coat? What do you pay janitors in Hungary?' She laughed. 'And would he be so bossy?' she asked wickedly. Vigadó gave her a shrewd look.

Divert him! her brain screamed. All she could manage was a simpering look of the utmost stupidity.

'Mimi, I do believe you're up to no good,' he said softly. The glint in his eyes looked lethal.

She did a mock 'who, little me?' expression because she was temporarily lost for words, her throat dry with fear. It could be her paranoia that sensed a sinister meaning behind that remark. Or... Her heart somersaulted. There was a chance, a remote chance, that he'd glimpsed her at the Frankfurt Book Fair in October.

Except... No! That had been the month she'd had long hair the colour of coal-tar—and had flown home early with flu. How could he recognise her? As a mere assistant to her last editor, she'd been one of the insignificant crowd, far from Vigadó's glittering entourage. And she'd been power-suited, immaculately made-up and wearing her frigid 'no-dice, hands-off' expression to keep three lusting authors at bay—and cursing her editor for entrusting them to her care.

Today, she was a blonde waif in cut-off, ragged shorts and a vest T-shirt and no make-up. He was being naturally suspicious, nothing more—and it wasn't surprising.

Cautiously, pretending to be fussing with her hair, she checked that no conker-coloured strands were escaping from Marilyn and then tried a resentful look on him. She had to fight this to the last ditch. It was all or nothing, sink or swim!

'I think you've got a nerve! I'm doin' everyone a favour, being here!' she declared stoutly.

'By waving your legs around enticingly? By launching yourself prettily into my arms?' he purred. It was like the caressing purr of a contented tiger, who was about to pounce... devour flesh and crunch bones!

'I told you. Me and my mates is decoratin' the place,' said Mariann, her perkiness not too successful because of the shake in her voice.

'I haven't seen them, but I'll agree that you decorate it very prettily,' he husked, his smoky accent deeper, more distracting than ever.

'Ta. Mind you, if I've still got me looks, it's no thanks to you,' she reminded him, putting him firmly in the wrong. 'It's a miracle I'm in one piece at all, what with you comin' in without warning.'

'Why is an English girl working as a decorator in Budapest?' he asked reasonably, but sardonically.

She simpered and launched into her story. 'I'm helpin' a couple of fellers I know. András and János. They're fittin' this job in as a favour. My mum's Hungarian. I got family over here,' she added truthfully.. 'Not a crime, is it? I got to eat, you know.' A mischievous impulse, born of desperation, made her launch into wild, inventive improvisation to establish her credentials before making a quick exit. 'I hope you know you've ruined me snake 'n' adder!'

His eyebrow rose quizzically, as well it might, she thought ruefully. And then she caught an excitement running through her veins and realised that playing risky games with the master of deception was rather enjoyable!

'Snake and...adder?' he drawled, his eyes narrowing.

'Cockney rhyming slang. Adder—ladder!' she explained sweetly, reasoning that it was rather unlikely that a Hungarian would be any kind of an expert.

'I'm fascinated by your barrow-boy wit!' he marvelled sarcastically. 'This is almost like *My Fair Lady*.'

'It is?' A little puzzled, Mariann let her eyelashes do a bit of overtime and prayed that that was admiration gleaming in his eyes.

'The simple Cockney girl in that particular musical turned into a raving beauty with a shrewd mind and a cut-glass accent,' he murmured and she smiled uncertainly.

'Oh, yeah. Audrey Hepburn. 'Scuse me,' she said, trying to ease out of his vice-like grip. Her hand looked decidedly white. Didn't he care about hurting women? 'I'd better give me ladder the once-over before I clean me brushes and go——'

'I was intending to give *you* the once-over, after your fall down the...' he paused, delicately, his mouth ironic '...adder!'

Mariann squirmed, not wanting to risk having a hands-on experience with Mr Bedroom Eyes himself and wondering what it would take to free herself.

'You tryin' to stop the blood flowing to me fingers?' she asked in pointed objection.

'Is that what I'm doing? Dear me! No wonder I'm known for breaking butterflies' wings on wheels,' he said in a low, unnervingly cruel undertone. He smiled unpleasantly, as though contemplating a few butterflies he'd destroyed, and Mariann's pulses lurched erratically. 'In certain circumstances, I use more force than necessary.'

'What circumstances?' she asked hoarsely.

His sharply sculptured lips curled into a calculating smile that coincided with the pressure of his hips against hers. 'When I'm aroused in one way or another.'

Aroused. Mariann swallowed hard. Was that anger or passion in his tone? She found it confusingly hard to tell. 'You come to the boil a bit quick!' she observed, her jaunty tone belying her fear.

'Depends how high the heat is turned up,' he said meaningfully. Mariann took the hint. She'd overdone it. This guy needed no encouragement for his sexual urge to take over. 'Now let's find out all about you, shall we?'

'I'm better at talkin' when I can breathe,' she husked. His thumbs were now massaging in an irritatingly rhythmic way over her flesh. Her tingling flesh. How could it tingle? she thought in mortification.

'And I'm better at getting information out of people when I have some kind of a hold over them,' he replied coolly.

She gasped at his blatant threat and decided it was time this trickster experienced a dirty trick or two in return. So she inhaled deeply. Vigadó's avid eyes fell to her T-shirt, which he watched with close interest as it rose beneath the strain of her lifting breasts.

And then, 'Read all about it!' she yelled, approximately two inches from his mesmerised face.

'What the devil——?' he roared, flinching violently.

She was free! 'Just checking my lungs work all right,' she said with bright innocence, taking a precautionary step or two nearer to the sanctuary of her outdoor clothes. A bit of bleached-blonde Marilyn slid seductively over one eye and she decided to leave it there. Her giggle surfaced at his pained expression. 'I haven't gone mad.' She grinned. 'That was——'

'I know,' he grated irritably. 'I've heard newspaper venders shouting that phrase in London. You bring the city sounds vividly back to me,' he added in icy sarcasm. 'You'll be doing the Lambeth Walk and impressions of Big Ben chiming next.'

She flung him an amused look and then her hand flew to her mouth to stifle a laugh. 'Oh, my!' she gasped. 'The paint's gone all over your nice pin-stripe!'

His gaze followed hers. 'Dammit!' he cried irritably, slipping his arms out of the expensive coat—mercifully untouched—and passing it imperiously to her. 'Look what you've done!'

Annoyed by his arrogant manner, she flung the coat in the general direction of his luggage and decided to have a dig at him. 'I didn't *ask* you to clutch me to you like a drownin' man grabbin' a lifebelt!' she argued indignantly.

'I was steadying you, after your launch into space,' he said in chilling tones. 'And I don't quite see myself as a drowning man.'

'Like a leech, then,' she said in a kindly way, because he was, having sucked the life blood from her boss's business.

His lips compressed. 'I think I'm beginning to understand what you're trying to convey,' he said caustically. And suddenly she saw that he looked tired, as though his journey had been a long one. Tired was good news, she thought, giving a sigh of relief. He'd be less of a menace. 'Have you got any turps?' he snapped.

'Sure,' she chirruped. She strode over to the tool box and solemnly handed him the bottle and some rags.

'You?' Curt and barely civil, he held out the bottle.

Thanking him politely, she took the worst of the stains off her shorts and then turned her attention to the spots on her legs, aware that his eyes kept flicking over to watch her movements. No harm in that. Plenty of men had ogled her legs before—but this time she felt more uncomfortable than usual so she gave one hasty, make-do rub and waited anxiously for the chance to leave.

Her heart was racing at an all-time high. That would be due to the danger, of course. But being found out was far less worrying than the air of sexual violence he was projecting. And also worrying was her extraordinary pagan response to it. What had happened to her immunity, her sense of the ridiculous when men became doe-eyed and panting?

Unfortunately for her, this guy was light-years away from being doe-eyed or panting. She, however, had felt alarmingly close to sinking, with a mindless sigh, into his arms! Extraordinary—and humiliating that she was reacting to his leader-of-the-pack attitude by virtually rolling over in submission!

She darted a quick, resentful glance at him and he looked away. His strong but deft fingers worked at the cloth, stretching it taut across his well-developed thighs. In fact, he was very muscular all over. And she wished he were a seven-stone weakling. She'd feel safer. At the moment, she felt as safe as a rabbit in a trap. She shivered—and knew with a sinking heart that she had to abandon her attempt and try again the next evening. All she needed was a good exit line.

CHAPTER TWO

IN FRUSTRATION, Mariann began to pack up her things. While Vigadó worked doggedly at the stains on his trousers, her mind drifted to another man who'd always dominated his environment: István, her sister's guy.

Fondly she contemplated the love-affair between István and Tanya—its ups and downs and eventual state of bliss. Whenever they'd looked into each other's eyes, her heart had contracted with a wistful envy. A mutual adoration like that was very moving. But bitter experience reminded her that men like him were rare, very rare, and the odds against falling in love with a man who met her special needs were virtually nil.

Mariann smiled gently. Nevertheless, their happiness had given her hope. Things *could* turn out well after difficulties. The thought inspired her to persevere with her daring plan.

Maybe Lionel's wife would return to him when she found out what a monster Vigadó really was. And Mary O'Brien—surely she wouldn't approve of the working methods of a brute whose sole motive was profit and damn the consequences? All they needed was Mary's secret address and they were home and dry.

'Is the paint coming off?' she enquired sweetly, her eyes lingering on the fine tailoring of his double-vented jacket and ferociously knife-edged trousers. Some of Lionel's authors had probably funded that suit!

'No. I hope the cleaners will have better luck. I hate waste,' he frowned, dropping the cloth rag in defeat. Foiled for once, and obviously hating the experience, he impatiently thrust back a hank of silky black hair that spoilt his impeccable appearance by daring to dip its wave on to his broad forehead.

24

'Disasters will happen. I'm sure it'll clean out,' she said soothingly, screwing the top back on the turps. 'Well, since you've arrived, I'll get out of your way now.'

'No, you won't! You'll tell me what you're planning first,' he said aggressively.

Mariann bit back her annoyance. 'You'll be dead surprised!' she promised wryly.

'You may be right, you may be wrong,' he said in an ice-splintered voice, and pushed his hands deep into the pockets of the sharply tailored jacket. 'Why don't you show me what you have in mind?'

Later! she thought, hugging her secret to herself. 'All right. Come and see.' Serenely content to be deceiving the dreaded monster, she knelt on the dustsheet beside the stack of paint tins.

'Here?' he asked lazily. 'How original.'

'You've got a dirty mind,' she reproved and grabbed a screwdriver, ignoring Vigadó's mock-exclamation of lecherous surprise and levering open a tin. She'd cheerfully directed the decorators to some interesting shades, just for fun, pretending that 'Viggy' would 'adore' her choice. And she'd enjoyed picking out the colours, majestically arranging for the bill to be sent to the Dieter Ringel office. 'Cantaloupe,' she pronounced proudly, showing him and revving up her cheery Cockney impersonation to full throttle. 'Bright, innit? Once it's slapped on the walls, you'll be real chipper! What do you think?'

'Can't say it's been one of my life's ambitions to work inside a melon,' he grunted, crouching beside her on the dustsheet. His hand stretched out to her discarded boiler suit beside him and fingered the emblem on the pocket reflectively. 'Kastély Huszár,' he mused, flicking a quick glance at Mariann's widening eyes. 'The hotel... How did you get hold of this?' he demanded sharply.

'Monogrammed, is it? That's posh for you!' she exclaimed.

And inwardly she groaned. Oh, help! He might know the countess! She made a mental note to ring István's mother and beg her not to reveal the family connection between them. Vigadó had to continue to believe that she was a simple, uncomplicated girl with nothing but empty space between her ears. If he got wind of the fact that she worked for a publisher——

'Are you having trouble formulating an answer?' he asked with sinister softness.

She blanched at the barbaric growl and sharpened her defences. Travel-weary he might be, but he was still more alert than most guys on their fifth cup of coffee.

'I didn't steal it, if that's what you're thinking,' she said, much on her dignity. 'The hotel supplied me with it,' she told him truthfully, rather pleased with her evasion. 'It's had a revamp,' she explained. 'Decorators everywhere.'

His head angled on one side. 'Everyone knows that. István Huszár and that English manager of his have made the hotel world-famous. You've worked there?' he probed, his glacial eyes boring into her soul.

Her heart began to thump. Lying didn't come easy to her, not after being brought up as a vicar's daughter! 'Did a few jobs,' she answered with a vigorous nod.

She smiled ruefully, thinking of when she'd helped her younger sister Sue to soothe a few hundred guests when their brother's wedding at the castle was dramatically cancelled. Or when she'd packed up the wedding presents. What a terrible day that had been! She could have wept—would have done—if Tanya hadn't been relying on her support. But the apparent disaster had brought Tanya and István together after years apart. Crises were often turning points.

Vigadó had stood up smoothly and was running incredulous eyes over her rather skimpily clad body. 'You're telling me you really are a decorator?' he asked in mild disbelief.

Mariann nodded blithely. After doing out their Devon home and her London friends' flats, she reckoned she could call herself that. 'That's right,' she said, thinking she was almost home and dry. A little more proof and he'd be convinced. Perhaps some colourful Cockney would help! 'Okey dokey, swivel your peepers this way——'

'Do you think,' he interrupted with a heavy sigh, 'that you could speak normal, *undecorated* English? I don't think my jet-lagged brain can cope with riddles.'

'I meant,' she said, cheerfully in command of the situation, 'for you to see what else we were doing.' Hoping to convince him by sheer self-assurance, she opened tins enthusiastically. 'Sultana skirting boards, flapjack ceiling and cane-sugar door panels with a cream surround. What do you think? Come on, be honest.' Mariann leapt up eagerly and her big smile broadened with delight at his shattered expression.

'Sounds like a greengrocer's shop in the West Indies,' he said caustically.

'Too right!' she sympathised. 'But there's colour charts for you,' she added, disclaiming all responsibility for the manufacturer's wild fantasies.

'This building is part of Budapest's historic Castle district,' he said wearily. 'You're working in what was once an eighteenth-century *salon*——'

'But the colours would look *stunning*!' she cooed.

'If this is a joke...' he began in stiff anger.

And she couldn't resist teasing him. 'Too unconventional? I thought it might be.' She sighed. 'Colours are supposed to reveal your inner character.' She eyed his suit with a professional air and let her gaze linger for a fraction too long on the lines of the beautiful body beneath. Wasted on a man like that...

'Enlighten me as to my character,' he said in clipped tones.

With pleasure! she thought. 'A guy who believes in straight-down-the-line commitment with no side-turnings, who's organised, ruthless to a fault, with no grey areas and no maybe,' she replied, sounding annoyingly husky. Conventional or not, he looked devastating. But then his earthy, raw sensuality would fight its way through anything he chose to wear. Stopping herself from wool-gathering, she waved an expressive hand towards her kaleidoscopic pile of clothes. 'What do mine say?'

He scanned the heap of reds, oranges and shocking pinks. 'They don't "say", they shout,' he grated in disapproval. 'They scream in raucous tones that you're as fast and as brash and as exciting as a fairground ride. A chameleon landing on those clothes would have a nervous breakdown.'

'You're funny!' she said in surprise. She was grinning good-naturedly at his assessment, not in the least bit bothered by it because she was proud of brightening a grey world, one hand jammed into her tiny waist above the womanly swell of her hip, her long legs and bare feet planted assertively apart.

'Hilarious. Stick your tongue out,' he commanded abruptly.

She almost obeyed. 'What?' She gaped in astonishment.

Suddenly he was as close as a tango dancer, looming over her, his snazzy-suited body authoritative and slightly menacing. A faint quiver of nerves rippled from her head to her toes. When his hand enclosed her bare arm like an iron manacle again, she wondered seriously whether she could actually get away with deceiving him. Those eyes of his could penetrate flaws inside iron girders.

'Stick your tongue out,' he repeated softly, and Mariann found herself swaying towards him, helplessly mesmerised by his smoulderingly sexy eyes.

She fought the urge to lift her mouth to Vigadó's inviting lips. He was even more wickedly sexy in the flesh than on paper, and of course that was how she had expected him to stay—a paper threat. It hadn't been her intention to be around when he arrived. If he'd stuck to his schedule, she thought resentfully, like any normal businessman, whose life was run by his Filofax, she would have extracted all the information she needed and been on her way before he ever knew he'd been invaded by decorators!

Or tempted her with his undeniably enticing mouth.

He lifted an insistent eyebrow. 'Your tongue,' he murmured.

Her head cleared a little. What could he do to it? she reasoned. Cut it off? Intrigued, she obliged, her eyes challenging his while she stuck out her tongue with an energetic thrust that turned the gesture into an out-and-out insult.

'Awrr righ'?' she enquired insolently.

A square of beautifully soft linen appeared in his hand and was gently moistened on her outstretched tongue while she covertly watched him—his long black lashes curling like a child's on his cheeks, his come-and-kiss-me mouth flowering before her eyes in a shockingly sensual enjoyment. Her heart began to thud faster and hastily she retracted her tongue, aghast that she was responding with such primitive eagerness to his compelling, raw sexuality.

She liked men. She liked kissing. Perhaps a cuddle. No more. More led to expectations, to commitment, to 'going steady'. And then obsessions, which she feared. Her sister Tanya's happiness, her mother's, father's, brother's—all had been nearly destroyed by obsession. And even the powerful István had been scarred by its denial. It was frightening, to be possessed by emotions.

To kiss this man would be an experience. But Vigadó gave out the impression that he'd never settle for less than complete surrender in return for his time and effort. Pity. She'd have liked to know what it felt like to have that amazingly carnal mouth on hers. It looked so wickedly, excitingly mobile...

She stiffened. He'd taken her face in one hand and slowly, solemnly rubbed at the paint splashes on her forehead, beneath the dip of her Marilyn waves. She jerked back and he continued on less dangerous areas of her brow. Snow from the sub-zero blizzard outside had dampened his hair and the freezing wind had given his face a healthy glow. He was so near, she mused, that she could feel the icy chill rising from his skin.

He smiled. It looked rather calculating to her and she sought to break the tension between them with a merry quip, but he got there first. 'Now we've cleared up the flapjack, we can proceed,' he murmured huskily. 'I wonder which of us is the hungriest? Who will devour whom?'

Mariann blinked. Did he mean the paint, or her? Dark eyes burned into hers. And then she felt the tip of his tongue touching her jawline and all hell broke loose inside her. Something odd had happened to her stomach. She shook her head slowly till she had some control over her voice—confused as to why her throat had closed up in collusion with her body.

'You can't eat me. You'd get poisoned,' she managed to croak out.

'Oh?' he murmured, his eyes mocking. 'Venom in your blood?'

'Lead in the paint,' she countered shakily.

He chuckled in a sinister way. 'Thanks for the warning,' he said silkily. 'I will look out for all the dangers when I'm tempted by beautiful and mysterious decorators putting in a bit of overtime.'

Mariann lowered her eyes modestly, her heart fluttering like crazy. There'd been a wealth of hidden meaning in his words. Tread carefully, she told herself. This man would be suspicious of his own mother.

'Flatterer!' she accused, feeling the desperation clouding her brain.

'Don't flirt,' he warned in a low tone. 'If I want a woman, I take her—without any need for coy messages of encouragement.'

She tried to force her throat to open again, deciding to make a stand. Because she mustn't fail! So a big smile and, 'Who's flirting?' she defied.

'You were,' he said curtly.

'Why would I do that?' she shrugged.

'Why indeed,' he stated starkly.

Mariann licked her lips nervously. Fencing with this Don Juan was a tactical mistake. She *must* make her exit soon, find a way to close that incriminatingly open filing cabinet and carry on the decorating farce for another day.

'If you don't like the colours,' she babbled, 'we could do mango and cocoa-brown with fudge...' The look in his eyes—beech-nut brown, or Havana? she wondered a little breathily—told her that it was time to stop. As usual she'd gone just a little too far. Her sense of fun had run away with her.

''Don't push it,' he said tightly. 'You're on dangerous ground.'

The beech-nut browns took another swift tour of her body. This time he made her feel so alarmingly naked that she wished she'd worn overalls. By now, the T-shirt was clinging rather indecently to her hot, damp breasts. The shorts weren't much better. When she'd cut the hems for ease of movement, she'd been sublimely indifferent to stares of the office staff—after all, she was playing a part and András and János knew better than to even glance below her neck, because she was 'Viggy's'. But this was Viggy himself. And he not only stared, he had a way of igniting her flesh and making it seem... more *fleshy*, more sexy than ever before. And that scared her.

'Sorry. Tell me what colours you want and I'll do them,' she said contritely, every inch of her aware of him—and hating the magnetic pull he was exerting over her. 'It's a shame,' she said, struggling for normality. 'I reckoned my scheme would look terrific——'

'You reckoned?' he interrupted sharply. 'My office manager should have made that kind of decision, not you. Sándor Millassin.'

'Antal,' she corrected, watching him closely.

'Of course,' he replied, as bland as milk. 'I forgot.'

She knew that was an out-and-out lie. Vigadó Gabór had the reputation of having a memory like an elephant. He was checking up on her! Must do better! she told herself angrily.

'Look, Antal was in a flap,' she said, giving him an edited version of the truth. In fact, it was because the manager had been in so much of a flap, with his office in such chaos and the dreaded Vigadó due that month, that her bluff had worked. Antal had swallowed everything she'd told him about 'Viggy's' generosity towards her. 'Apparently you'd suddenly decided to switch your headquarters to Budápest and he wanted everything to look smart for you. He was far too busy making offers for the building next door and ordering equipment to bother with minor details like colour charts.'

Vigadó wandered to the window and stared out at the broken ice patterning the Danube below. The converted mansion stood high on a dramatic rocky outcrop above the city. Now the blizzard had stopped it was possible to see the whole panorama of the snow-blanketed city across the white-flecked river.

Mariann edged a little closer to glimpse the dazzling beauty of romantic Budapest. Her face softened. There was the vast Gothic parliament building, its severe façade turned into an elaborately decorated wedding-cake by the snow icing. And on its balcony, she mused, a Hungarian Prime Minister had once made a plea for freedom from Soviet occupation. How awful, to have been oppressed——

'What's the name of the people you work for?' asked Vigadó with a sudden verbal lunge.

She blinked, dragging her mind back to a present-day oppressor, and told him. He checked the phone book, wrote down the number on a pad and faced her again, the jet-black hair stark against the leaden skies, his face a dark, unreadable blur in the fading light. 'I'll ring them in the morning.'

'No point. They'll be here,' she said, worrying that he'd find out someone had impersonated him.

'Why aren't the men working overtime? Why you?'

Suddenly Mariann felt trapped. His body language was telling her that she was being very astutely judged and found wanting. 'I—I badly need the money,' she said huskily. 'I begged and coaxed them to let me carry on.'

'Clever.'

She thought so. Living on her wits was becoming a way of life and life was a series of opportunities. 'We're doing a good job, and doing it fast. We'll be out of your way before you know it.' True! He scowled at her and stayed silent. 'Well?' she asked anxiously.

'No, it isn't "well". Far from it. Get out of here,' he said with a sudden, brutal finality. 'Don't bother to come back. I'll get my own man in.'

Mariann stared at him in dismay. Her careful plans, all her work, had come to an abrupt end! She'd failed! Helplessly she watched Vigadó sling his coat over his shoulder and pick up his briefcase. His dark, steely eyes flicked back contemptuously to her as he paused in the door that led to the next office. She froze.

'I told you to go!'

'But you can't mean that! What about my mates?' she wailed, moving forward to head him off. The image of the open cabinet burned in her mind.

'For God's sake!' he snapped. 'Don't you have any sense of self-preservation? Don't you know what a dangerous man I am?' His voice became a low, savage growl, his eyes petrified her with their intense black anger. 'Stay,' he said menacingly, 'and you risk more than a little damage to that beautiful face of yours.'

Her eyes flipped automatically to his scar while his glance swept from her toes to her head, slowly, measuring her inch by inch. With every flicker of his thick, dark lashes, Mariann felt weaker, the caress of his eyes on her lips making them part, the contempt, when their eyes finally met, rocking her on her heels. And it was the first time that she'd ever felt so scared for her own safety that she was close to being physically sick.

'You have ten seconds to move, two minutes to clear the mess!' rapped Vigadó.

'Impossible! I need to clean——'

'*Go*!'

There was no sense in inviting an explosion of that simmering temper. Mariann sullenly shrugged her shoulders. 'You're the boss.' What on earth was she going to do? 'I think you've dropped your wallet or something,' she said, pointing back vaguely to her heaped clothes. When he grunted and strode over to check, she slipped past him into the next office and quietly pushed the cabinet shut.

'Nothing there,' he said softly, returning. 'Now what are you doing?'

'Checking there's nothing of mine in here,' she said breathlessly.

Cold and hard, the sinister dark eyes lingered on hers for a few scary seconds. 'I believe everything in there belongs to me,' he said tightly, and strode to the desk, sifting through the mail as if she didn't exist any more.

Thinking savagely that half the authors in that cabinet rightly belonged to their original publishers and not him at all, she stalked out, racking her brains for a way out. It seemed awful just to walk away and admit defeat. He shouldn't always get whatever he wanted, she thought resentfully. He bullied people, using whatever means he could—power, the threat of violence, sex. Angrily she pushed cleaning rags into a carrier bag and wrapped the roller.

She didn't want him to win. She never abandoned anything she'd set out to do. It had been so easy for him, to arrive, snap out a few questions and decide he didn't want to be bothered with a perfectly good gang of decorators.

A small voice inside her urged her to go, that arguing with him would be imprudent and staying would be risky. But she'd always been more stubborn than wise, *making* things work for her. Throughout her life, her policy had always been to go that extra mile, push harder, further than other people to reach her goal and never to show weakness.

That was how, she mused, she had won the reputation of never being troubled, of always being happy and sunny. Even her family believed that. But early on she'd seen that they'd had enough troubles of their own without hearing about hers—and they, like everyone else, had come to see her as the one bright and cheering ray of sunshine in their lives.

Only her younger sister, Sue, knew that there were dark days too. That the constant effort to show the expected sparkling face had become part of a role she didn't always want to play.

Mariann grimaced and slowly dunked her brushes in the turps jar before suspending them in their clips. Her elder sister Tanya was warm, motherly and deeply committed to them all. John, well, he was a kid brother, eager, enthusiastic, romantic. Sue was sensible and down-to-earth.

Smiling, Mariann thought that it was odd how easily she'd drifted into being the glamorous, carefree one. Men went out with her for those qualities—her ability to enjoy life, have fun, make them laugh—and not because she looked homely or could bake feather-light sponges.

Sometimes she wondered if anyone would ever see deeper than the external face she showed the world. But when she'd once revealed some of her real self, everyone had thought she was fooling around and had laughed at her hesitant confidences.

A smile, a quip, a witty remark...they'd never wanted any more. And increasingly everyone had come to think that she was so tough, she could work miracles. Like now. She straightened, her eyes on Vigadó's dauntingly broad back. 'England expects...' she thought, and smiled wryly.

And then a thought popped suddenly into her head uninvited: how lovely it would be to have a relationship with a man who had a stronger will than she! Mariann grinned. No, it would be awful! Too many fights! Talking of which, this Vigadó was one guy she *didn't* want to get the better of her!

Action stations! Re-form! Charge!

Giggling to herself, she padded over to the open door of the next office, watching his body move lithely around as he emptied his briefcase.

He hadn't noticed her, her bare feet making no sound on the dustsheets. On the brink of speaking, she checked herself. He'd stiffened all his muscles in tension. Bending over his case, he picked up a framed photograph of a woman and stared at it. Slowly and deliberately, he pushed it back into the briefcase with a gesture that suggested he loathed the very sight of the woman.

Vigadó's wife? she wondered. It hadn't been Liz—Lionel's wife—because the photo she'd seen had shown her boss with a dark woman. The one in Vigadó's photograph was ash-blonde. He squared his shoulders as though coming to a decision and turned. Her eyes widened at the expression of dark despair that filled his face with a vulnerable, human quality she hadn't seen before.

But instantly his face tautened into a mask, smoothing away the bitter sorrow of his mouth, the bleakness in his eyes, the heart-tugging lines of strain.

Mariann was fascinated. He did have doubts, worries, problems, like normal men! And that meant he was accessible. There was something inside him she could appeal to if necessary. It gave her hope.

'You still here?' he shot.

Bullies backed down if you stood up to them. She'd known enough men who'd grabbed her and crumbled when she'd assaulted them with scathing words. And this one, apparently, had a wounded core. Inspiration came to her.

'Just wanted to say that you'll be hearing from me.' Stiff and proud, she turned, collected the two largest paint tins and carried them to the outer door.

'You're not trying to coax me to let you stay or... anything else?' he asked in surprise, stepping forward to stare after her.

'No. See you in court,' she answered crisply.

'Court?' He gave a small, incredulous laugh.

'Yup.'

The laugh came again. 'Suing?' She didn't answer. 'Did you have a written agreement, a contract?'

'Yes,' she said, unperturbed. There had been a generous price for the job and she knew there'd been a backhander arranged for Antal. Disapproving of such corruption, she'd pretended not to see the money change hands, telling herself that Vigadó cheated so many people, he shouldn't be surprised if his staff cheated him too. She prayed her father would never find out what she was doing.

'I hope you've got a work permit,' he snapped.

'No.'

'Well! You personally don't seem to be on very firm ground,' he said scathingly. 'How are you intending to sue me? By claiming sexual harassment?'

At the low, meaningful probe, she gave him a mysterious smile and turned her back on him. 'Now. Where did I put my flat brush...?'

'Try a charge like that and my lawyers will expose your background and your case will fall through,' he said contemptuously.

'I'm not trying it,' she said, calmly taking one ladder at a time to the corridor outside.

Vigadó moved further into the room. 'Then what the hell are you playing at?' he asked with exasperation steaming from every word.

Mariann grinned to herself. She'd successfully captured his attention. Tycoons hated mysteries and they had to be in control. 'I'm not playing. It's not a game to me. I'm trying to make a livelihood,' she said, weaving elements of truth into her answer. How could this be a game, when her job as editor depended on it? 'I care passionately about my work. I'm just starting out and I need to get more experience——'

'You will,' he drawled. 'With a body like that, you will, I can assure you.'

She ignored his taunt. 'You have no reason to break the contract,' she said with dignity. 'We've worked darn hard, hour after hour without proper breaks, to get the job done fast. My arms ache, I've been inhaling paint fumes so I feel nauseous, I've spilled paint all over me and I'm fed up with your bad-tempered behaviour just because you turn up earlier than expected yet you want everything to be perfect!' She risked an indignant glare. 'Oh, no. Neither I nor the firm will be suing you!'

'No?' he prompted, his brows drawn together in puzzled lines.

'No. you'll be suing me,' she said simply. And she picked up her Thermos flask and sandwiches with a purposeful air.

'Wait a minute! I'm riveted. Tell me why and maybe we can short-circuit this proposed court appearance,' he said drily.

'Well, I'll be telling my story to a newspaper, of course!' she said, wide-eyed and artless.

'You'll what? Which story?' He'd taken two quick strides and caught her beneath her armpits, lifting her in the air till she was level with his thunderous face. 'Which story?' he snarled.

'Put me down and I'll tell you!' she gasped. 'Unless you want a Thermos and a packet of cheese and pickle smashed over your head!'

'Your hand wouldn't get that far,' he growled, but dumped her roughly on the floor nevertheless. 'Speak.'

She stood her ground, whereas she would have preferred to move back from the alarmingly angry rise of his expanded chest. 'I'd tell them the story I've just told you. How hard I've tried to please their home-grown whiz-kid's imperious demands, slaving my fingers to the bone, going without sleep——' She caught a malevolent flicker in his eyes and hastily scrapped the rest of her litany. 'Basically, I'm going to appeal to the Hungarian people's sense of fair play, and their empathy with people who work long hours, and tell them how badly you treat your employees——'

His hands stayed her. 'Oh, no. I won't let you do that. There are enough lies flying around about me as it is. I'm impressed,' he said slowly. 'No wonder you landed the job.' Mariann kept her eyes lowered and held her breath. 'What a clever woman you are! You do know how to get what you want,' he murmured, tucking blonde strands behind her ear. 'That kind of perseverance and dedication deserves some kind of reward.'

'Oh!' He was weakening! 'You're so right! I *am* relieved you see it my way at last!' she cried happily, deciding to flatter him. 'I knew there was a decent heart inside that ruthless exterior——'

'Please,' he protested mockingly. 'You'll ruin my reputation for tyranny.'

'I won't tell,' she grinned. 'And...I'll do my best——'

'I'll make sure you will,' he said softly and smiled a thin, unnervingly venomous smile as though he meant to examine every inch of paintwork and pronounce judgement on it. 'I can well imagine that you're very good at your job. You can understand my suspicion. You're the most unlikely-looking decorator I've ever seen.'

'I know. It's the outfit, isn't it?' she said innocently, catching his glance wandering hungrily over her bare legs again. The sultry expression in his dark eyes suggested he wanted to work his way up from her feet, tasting every inch of skin. She quivered and quickly suppressed the deliciously curling sensation that had come with that thought.

'And your reason for dressing like that is...?'

'Sweat!' she said, hoping to kill all thoughts of sex— her own thoughts as well as his—with her bombshell directness. 'If I don't strip off the layers, I get overheated. Your offices are awfully hot with the central heating turned up all day and it's too bitter outside to open the windows. I like fresh air. I'm a country girl myself, you see.'

'Is that so?' he stated flatly. 'I had no idea the East End of London was considered to be the country.'

She gazed at him in consternation and then recovered herself. 'It isn't. My family live in Devon,' she explained hastily. 'Dad retired there.'

'Is that how you got the job at Kastély Huszár?' he queried in a tone of mild curiosity. 'The English manager comes from Devon, I believe.'

She blinked. 'Yes,' she admitted, wondering what Vigadó would do if he knew 'the English manager' was her brother John! 'You have to use all the contacts you can,' she said disarmingly.

'No doubt you've made some worthwhile contacts with my staff too,' he purred.

'Well, you see me here, so I suppose I did. So we can carry on working?' she said, checking, just to be sure.

'Shall we say...I would like you to turn up to-morrow?' he replied carefully.

'Oh! Wonderful! Th-ta!' she cried in delight.

'Not dressed like that, though,' he drawled. 'I'm sure my staff would be delighted if you clambered up and down ladders in those clothes, but I'd prefer them to keep their eyes and minds on their work.'

'OK. I'll wear overalls,' she assured him earnestly. 'I won't even sing. Can't say fairer than that!'

'I was surprised to hear singing,' he mused. 'Most people only sing in the bath.'

Something in his tone brought a warm curling glow to her insides. She knew enough about men to realise that he'd look fabulous nude, the water gleaming on those pecs and biceps... Her muscles tensed at the disturbing and tantalising image of soap-suds gliding down his narrow hips and she ruefully gathered up her hysterical hormones and confined them to barracks again.

'I sing in the bath too. Got to keep our plastic ducks amused, haven't we?' She grinned, but her voice was croakier than it should be.

His slow glance sent unwanted shock-waves up and down her spine. 'I prefer something a little more tactile,' he replied huskily.

Several hormones went AWOL again. 'Uh-huh. Loofahs.' She nodded sagely and was rewarded with a flash of amusement in his dark eyes.

'I do believe,' he murmured softly, 'that my jet-lag has suddenly vanished.'

'Well, isn't that nice?' she cried merrily and then her brows drew together in a dark line. 'Did you say jet-lag?' she queried in surprise. 'Don't whiz-kids fly Concorde?'

'Naturally. But back-to-back meetings in Sydney, Hong Kong and New York take their toll nevertheless.'

Her hazel eyes were filled with well-simulated awe. 'I've never talked to a tycoon like you before,' she said in admiration, her mind working furiously. He'd relaxed a little and seemed willing to talk at last. She was more than willing to listen while she finished clearing away because she might break down the barriers between them. 'Here. Have some coffee. A cheese and pickle sandwich,' she offered, generously passing him the remains of her lunch before ferrying the equipment back into the room. 'And tell me what you *do* at these meetings,' she said earnestly as she did so. 'Do you talk about sales figures and thump the table and gee people up?'

Declining the food, he hesitated before answering and, hoping to encourage him, she adopted an attitude of fascinated attention. 'Mainly we were talking about authors,' he replied casually.

Her body tensed with excitement. 'Gosh! Isn't that thrilling? It's one heck of a glamorous world. I read historical novels,' she told him eagerly, deliberately not choosing to mention the subject she was *most* interested in. 'Do you do those?'

'We "do" everything.' His dark eyes flickered. 'Travel books, reference, mystery and suspense, romance... sagas...'

To Mariann, there seemed to be an increasing tension between them, a waiting, as if each of them was assessing the other, circling, throwing a wary punch or two. And she knew she dared not pursue the avenue he'd left open to her. Every fibre of her being might be directed towards tracing saga-writer Mary O'Brien but this wasn't the way to do it. She'd have to be patient till tomorrow.

'Must make your eyes tired,' she said sympathetically, 'doin' all that readin'.' He smiled faintly. 'Speaking of tired, my mum said I should never outstay my welcome so I'd better get my things on.'

'I'll see you tomorrow.' He shut the door and she was left gazing at its heavy panels, feeling a sense of anticlimax. It had all been easy after all. Too easy? Her brow furrowed in anxiety.

Trudging through the snow back to the Budapest Hilton a short distance away, she mentally reviewed her position. She *thought* she'd allayed his suspicions, but wasn't sure. In the morning, she'd have to ask her two fellow decorators not to refer to the fact that she was 'Viggy's' girl.

Despite her predicament, she had to smile. This was the kind of crazy, impossible situation she loved as a challenge to her ingenuity—though several times she'd felt she'd been sailing a little close to the wind!

Lionel rang her and she told him what had happened. 'The next night, I'll get that address if I have to set the office on fire and stay on to ransack the cabinet while the flames are leaping about my ears!' she joked.

'Do that,' he said hysterically. 'I can't hold the bank longer than a couple of days!'

'Tell them Mary's as good as yours again,' she said gently, worried about Lionel's state of mind. 'Rely on me, I'll do everything I can.'

They all worked hard the next day—she, her two 'mates' and everyone in the office. Vigadó had either worked all night or had begun at some ungodly hour because when she arrived at eight he was already into a third cup of coffee and barely looked up when she was let in by the janitor.

The reaction of the staff when they saw their boss had arrived unexpectedly was quite amusing. Horror, panic, then a frantic appearance of work—as in a speeded-up film. And Vigadó had said virtually nothing to produce this effect. This was all on the strength of his formidable reputation.

Beneath the boiler suit she boiled. But she didn't dare strip off. Not with eagle eyes flicking her the odd glance every now and then. So she slaved on the ceiling while her colleagues did the more difficult gloss-work, her neck aching more and more as the endless hours wore on.

Tonight, she told herself. She'd get those records tonight. And prayed that he'd go to bed early after such a long day.

'Staying on *again*?'

The hairs on the back of her neck lifted. He'd crept up behind her. 'Just want to finish this bit of cantaloupe,' she said, 'and you can decide if you like it or not when you get the whole effect.'

'I think I'll call it a day,' he murmured, jingling coins in the pocket of his dark grey business suit. She stiffened. Or were they keys? 'Perhaps I'll decide tomorrow.'

Terrific! 'If you like,' she said politely. And he'd gone. Mariann waited for her thudding heart to slow down and listened. He was slowly walking up the marble stairs to the penthouse apartment above. A few agonising moments later, she let out a long breath of relief and put the roller down on the huge tin.

Silently she slipped into the office he'd been using. It was dark and she couldn't find the keys anywhere. It was several seconds before she realised that they were no longer in the drawer. Closing her mind to the fact that they *were* in his pocket, she whirled and heaved ineffectually at the drawers of the filing cabinet. Locked. So she methodically worked through everything in the office but found no keys of any kind.

Leaning against the cabinet, she forced her brain to come up with ideas. The keys were almost definitely in his possession. Either tonight or some other night she'd have to get them. They'd be still in his pocket, or on his dressing-table if he changed from the formal suit into something more casual for the evening.

Mariann bit her lip. But how to lay her hands on them? This wasn't some backwoods lad she could fool. However...people said she was sexy. Her sex-appeal had always been a terrible burden and she'd never turned on its full voltage because of the trouble it might get her into. So far she'd always had a tongue sharp enough to cut groping men down to size. She knew exactly how to cool their ardour. Maybe this was the time to test her quick wit to the limit. If she could get into Vigadó's apartment, perhaps find some excuse...

She gulped. It would be a case of getting close enough to pick his pocket, or search the bathroom and his bedroom. Risky. But she didn't have any choice. Lionel was relying on her.

Could she be frightened of something? Scream, run upstairs and claim an intruder had come in...? No, the janitor would come running. And a straightforward, Can I see your etchings? approach would get her into his bed quicker than she could say Picasso. But if she were in trouble...

She remembered how paint had stained his last pair of trousers and he'd been fastidious enough to get annoyed. Her face lit up with a broad grin. If he was still wearing the charcoal-grey gear, she could ruin it and make sure he removed it. If not, she could get into his bathroom by the same plan that had formed in her mind.

'You're brilliant!' She giggled to herself.

Hurrying back to where she'd been working, she impatiently tore off her boiler suit, pushed the roller off the tin and slopped cantaloupe paint down her shorts. It slid in satisfying melony rivers all down her bare legs. Perfect!

Trying not to laugh, she allowed it to stain her golden skin for a few moments, let out a loud yell, paused, and ran up the marble steps to Vigadó's apartment.

CHAPTER THREE

VIGADÓ had changed into casual beige trousers and
jacket, as she'd hoped, and cradled a drink in his hand.
It worried her that he didn't look surprised to see her
at all.

'An accident!' she wailed, displaying her legs.

'Yes?'

'My legs are turning marmalade!'

'Yes.'

Men must have been kidding her about her sex-appeal!
she thought irritably. Here she was, all legs and heaving
bosoms, and throwing herself on his mercy, and he
wasn't affected at all! Her lip quivered mutinously. 'I
can't put my clothes on over this!' She waggled a bright
knee about. He didn't even look down. So she caught
his arm and moved in closer, looking up at him with
wide, pleading eyes. 'I know it's a cheek, but can
I . . . could I use your shower?'

'There's a staff washroom downstairs.' He made to
close the door.

Her knee jammed in it quickly and she leaned all her
weight against it, finding herself almost falling into the
apartment when he let the door go. 'There's no scrubbing
brush,' she explained. 'I've run out of turps——'

'You want to use my bathroom.'

'Yes,' she said demurely, hoping he'd dumped his suit
there.

His mouth looked rather cynical. 'I suppose you know
what you're doing.'

It seemed to Mariann that his voice was charged with
husky indolence, as though he had plans, and she felt
the nerves curling her toes. 'Of course,' she answered,
not at all sure.

'Come in. I'll show you the bathroom.'

45

'Thanks,' she said brightly. 'I'd better get that loofah workin' smartish!' she joked, a little worried about his motives. 'In there? I can manage from here.' Accelerating her pace, she strode into the bathroom and made to slam the door—but he was there, behind her. 'I can manage,' she said again, pointedly, and scanned the room. No discarded clothes. Darn!

'Please allow me.' Reaching past her, he turned on the bath taps and sprinkled exotic oils into the water. His courtesy was all wrong but she'd known the risk she'd be running. Searching for some diversionary remark, she leant forward and let her fingers ripple through the scented water. 'Smells nice. Like Christmas pudding.'

'Perfumes and spices of the Orient,' he murmured, his voice betraying a suppressed laugh.

Her spirits lifted considerably. If she could keep him amused, she'd be all right. 'That explains it. My first time in a sunken bath, you know!' she confided, trying to sound dazzled by the experience. 'I won't hog it for long. Please carry on with whatever you were doing——'

'Thank you. I will. I was about to have a bath and turn in for the night,' he said smoothly.

'Oh! Yes... well, I expect you're still tired from all those meetings and never sitting down——'

'What was that you said?'

She ground her teeth with self-anger. There was no reason why she should know that he never allowed people to sit on chairs at his meetings! Who'd tell a decorator's assistant that? 'Lucky guess. I can see you now,' she said, her eyes glazing with a far-away look, 'striding up and down, telling everyone what to do while they sit *riveted*. Now,' she continued, turning off the taps and anxious to escape his interrogation, 'I'll be quick,' she promised breathily. 'Then you can come in——'

'Can I just clarify this?' he said silkily. 'You're inviting me to have a bath with you?'

'A—a bath?' Shocked, she swallowed away the lump in her throat. 'I—I——'

'You're very generous. Thank you. I accept,' he drawled, loosening his tie.

Mariann's eyes grew enormous. 'Whoa there!' she rasped. 'I meant I'd clean myself up quickly so you could settle in for a quiet night!'

'Ye-e-es.'

'No!' she squealed. 'Not with me! You're obviously exhausted and——'

'You think I'm too tired to do you justice?' he enquired silkily. The tie now hung loose, his fingers busy with the top button of his shirt. 'I'm never too tired for a beautiful woman...Mimi.'

Her heart thudded loudly, her eyes mesmerised by the gleaming perfection of his tanned throat. She was in trouble. 'On second thoughts,' she said huskily, 'I don't think this bath is a good idea after all. I've read enough novels with steamy bath scenes,' she muttered, trying a rather nervous joke.

'Don't tease,' he husked. 'I'm far too busy to spare time to run after you. You're a very sexy woman. And perhaps in need of money? I think we could come to some satisfactory arrangement and put this event on a business footing.'

Hardly able to believe what he was proposing, she stared in astonishment, her hazel eyes darkening with anger at the insult. His mouth looked ready to ravish hers, his gaze compelling, hungry, sending a wash of heat through her. And, to her alarm, she realised that her hesitation had encouraged him to slide his hand around her small waist. The softness of her hip. The...the top of her thigh!

She dithered in an agony of suspense as his fingers played expertly with the soft curves of her buttocks. Now what? She could hit him with all her strength and lose all chance of getting Mary's address. Or... The delay was beginning to take its toll. Vigadó knew how to caress a woman for maximum effect. And, to her horror, she was quivering in feminine delight, her head tipping back, her eyelids closing...

'No,' she said thickly, mesmerised by his come-to-bed eyes, all jokes, all clever retorts dying on her trembling lips.

'Satisfyingly unconvincing. Start without me. I'll be with you in a moment,' he husked, slapping her bottom playfully.

'Ouch!' she yelped. With some regret, she resisted the urge to employ her elbow with equal abandon. 'I'm not——!' she began hoarsely.

'No games,' he growled. 'I haven't the time. What about just getting on with it? Stop playing let's pretend. We'll skip all the preliminaries, shall we, and go straight to bed?'

Mariann was stunned into silence. Never, in the whole of her admittedly proposition-packed life, had she ever heard such a cold-blooded, matter-of-fact suggestion! And with the anger came a furious contempt for a man who used women purely to relieve his sexual appetite. She simply gaped at him.

'You seem annoyed that I've come straight to the point,' he drawled. 'I do hope you haven't been asked to play the 'string him along, he likes being teased' game. I'd prefer us to get it over with.'

Her jaw dropped even further. '*You—you*——!'

'You're busy, I'm busy, why waste time?' he said with staggering logic. 'Now to business. My taste is to make love in unusual places, and to incorporate plenty of action. I'm a very *physical* lover. I do hope you're supple—you've read the *Kama Sutra*, I imagine?'

'I... You... *No!*' she squeaked in horror.

'No, you're not supple, or... Oh, Mimi, you surprise me, a girl like you! Surely you're not conventional? Or...expecting to get away with a quickie in bed?' he mocked, and gave a sorrowful shake of his head. 'I was thinking of something much longer-lasting—and somewhere interesting for my jaded appetite. I'd want my money's worth, you see. You'd have to work hard. Dear, oh, dear!' He sighed. 'It seems whores aren't what they used to be!'

'*Whores*?' yelled Mariann.

'OK. Call-girls if you prefer. Let's not offend your dignity.' He shrugged sardonically.

'I don't know what you're suggesting!' she cried indignantly, clutching her body as if that would protect her from him.

'You women have to protest, don't you? I'm trying to make your job easier,' he said calmly. 'Think of it as cutting a few corners. You can eliminate all the preliminary vamping and move straight to the first position.' He smiled. 'Shall we discuss what that's to be? Upright, prone——'

'No!' she raged.

'It's to be a surprise?' he said, with a wolfish grin. Or was that laughter? she wondered, mystified. 'Fine by me. Now to details.' His eyes flickered, his mouth quivered, and she wasn't sure if it was in amusement or desire. 'It doesn't look as though you've brought any bondage gear but I think we can improvise with a couple of my ties and a belt or two—the bed's certainly strong enough and we can tie you to the bedpost——'

'Stop! Stop! You leave me speechless!' she gasped, scarlet with mortification, blocking her mind to thoughts of Vigadó's elaborate, inventive sex-life. He *was* teasing her, wasn't he? 'Why are you saying this?'

'Because I think you should have some inkling of what you've let yourself in for,' he said smoothly.

'Please!' she breathed, horrified, and licked her lips nervously at his sinister smile. 'You have absolutely no reason to believe I'm on the game!' she wailed, furious that his misunderstanding was thwarting her purpose.

'I wouldn't be too sure of that,' he said quietly. 'But tell me something that's been intriguing me: have I been a tremendous influence on you?' When she blinked, perplexed, he smiled nastily. 'Am I your Professor Higgins?'

'This is all a dream,' she breathed weakly. 'I don't——'

'My fair lady,' he mocked, 'your Cockney accent seems to have disappeared entirely.'

She stared at him dumb-struck. For a moment she considered denying his observation, but the hard, grim line of his mouth dissuaded her. She'd been rumbled. 'Oh. You're pretty smart,' she ground out sullenly.

'That's never been in dispute.' He waited, apparently quite relaxed, for an explanation. And then she realised that he wasn't relaxed at all. The body might be in a nonchalant pose, but he was like a coiled spring, leaning in her direction.

And power-crazy men never liked being deceived, she knew that, so she struggled to find an excuse, cursing him for knowing enough about British accents to expose her lie. 'I was doing OK till you made me cross,' she said resentfully.

'That's how I operate,' he drawled, 'by getting people to let down their guard. They're easier to dominate that way.'

She glared. 'It's not very nice.'

'But it gets results,' he observed coldly. 'And if you want your story to stick another time, I'd advise you to invest in some better glue.'

She blinked, confused. 'Pardon?'

He scowled. 'Your wig's crooked.'

'Oh, no!' Her heart beating painfully, Mariann slowly reached up and removed the wig. Not a muscle moved in his face; even his eyes were without expression as they studied her dark auburn hair and she was incapable of stopping herself from running her hands through the elegant, fashionably cut bob.

'It's beautiful,' he growled softly and she paused in the middle of shaking her silky hair back into place, her eyes widening at his remark. 'I wonder why you would ever choose to be blonde, when your own hair is the colour of polished mahogany?'

She blinked at his flattering description and thought hard. 'I—I wasn't getting anywhere as a brunette,' she said shakily. 'Oh, no, don't misinterpret that!' she cried quickly, seeing an ominous tightening of his jaw. She had to get his mind off bed and bondage. And floors. Or...wherever! 'Men—men prefer b-blondes,' she stammered. 'I mean...blondes stand out in a crowd. They get noticed; it's a fact of life, like it or loathe it, and personally I loathe it——'

'Because you hate men being boringly predictable?' he drawled.

'Yes,' she said guardedly. Was *he*? She wasn't sure now. She still didn't know if he was kidding her or serious. 'Well, I'd paid a lot for this haircut——'

'It shows,' he acknowledged. 'You must earn good money.'

'It was for a family wedding,' she explained honestly, relieved that she was leading him away from thoughts of seduction. 'It does look classy, I know. I was finding it hard to get a job. So...' she did her best to look rueful and stay close to the truth '...I put on Marilyn and—bingo!—the decorating firm took me on!'

'Marilyn.' His mobile mouth was on the move and Mariann hoped against hope that she'd disarmed him. There was certainly a different light in his eyes, though, far from being friendly, it was turning into an intense silver glitter. She squirmed uncomfortably beneath its third-degree burn. 'You have Hungarian features,' he mused. 'Beautiful bone-structure. Exotic eyes...'

'I told you, my late mother was Hungarian,' she explained brightly, breaking in on his throaty compliments. His accent became more pronounced whenever he said anything sensual. It was driving her crazy. She took a deep breath to lessen the warm glow filling her body. 'That's why I came over here. I'd always wanted to see Mother's homeland and delve a bit into my roots, especially as my brother and sister were over here,' she said, being as chatty as she could. 'We didn't know much about our background as children——'

'Your brother and sister?'

Her face softened and lost its wariness. 'John and Tanya—and I have a younger sister, Sue. Mum came to England as a young woman and we were brought up in Widecombe-in-the-Moor. It's a small Devon village.' He greeted that confidence with silence, the warm affection in her voice ringing in her own ears.

'So you never were familiar with the East End of London,' he murmured, his eyes narrowed.

'Oh. Not really. Other than ... I had a job there once. I—I didn't tell you an out-and-out lie,' she said, shame-faced. 'I put on the accent for my own benefit. It sort of went with the wig, you see, and reminded me that I was a blonde,' she said lamely. And that she was supposed to be the unkindly stereotyped dumb blonde and not make smart remarks.

She hung her head. Now she was explaining, she was ashamed of her behaviour. But Lionel had told her that she was too threatening as she was; that her air of authority and competence could jeopardise her hopes of getting into the office. And, because he'd been almost hysterically insistent, she'd agreed. Pity. She should have gone with her initial instincts.

'You thought that the men you met would be more receptive to a beautiful, idiot blonde who fluttered her lashes and pouted a pair of lush, promising lips at him,' Vigadó said, his voice laced with a lingering huskiness.

Mariann frowned. 'It sounds rather calculating——'

'It does. I imagine you are. Though ... you're not an airhead, are you?' His faint smile shattered the intense silver light of his eyes into faceted diamonds.

'No, I'm not!' she said cautiously. 'Or a whore. Or a call-girl. I don't even know for sure what a call-girl does.'

'They're for hire,' he said in clipped tones. 'They are paid a lot of money to play with some conviction any part the hirer wishes. Slave, whore, dominator, adoring companion. They've learnt how to please men, how to flatter, to play up to their insecurities and make them think they're God.'

Her contempt for him deepened. He knew so much about the subject that she supposed he must resort to that kind of shallow sexual encounter whenever he travelled. What a terrible life.

'I'm not a call-girl,' she insisted quietly. 'I know I was deceiving people,' she continued in a troubled tone, 'and I wish it hadn't been necessary. I do realise it's difficult for you to understand why I did so. But you don't know what it's like to need work——'

'I do,' he said softly.

'Oh. Yes.' She'd forgotten that he'd clawed his way to the top. Her mouth turned down. He'd done that by developing his body till he was an irresistible hunk of highly toned, state-of-the-art muscle and had turned his sinister good looks to good use by parading them before an heiress. And he was accusing *her* of using her sexual assets! 'Then you'll know when you get desperate you'll go to any lengths,' she reminded him defiantly.

'Any lengths?' he murmured, his eyebrow querying.

'Not the lengths you were thinking,' she said coldly. 'You don't think much of women, do you?'

'I've met far too many who fall woefully short of the ideal,' he growled.

'You can't blame me for that!' she said irritably. 'You mustn't think I'd sell my body! I don't even fool around with men's feelings! If I flirt, I do it openly and it's obvious that's what I'm doing because it's always over-the-top fun that no one could misinterpret. And if a man gets the wrong idea I put him right immediately.'

'As you did with me?' he countered sarcastically.

Her face went scarlet. 'All right, I admit I didn't slap you down when you richly deserved it! That was a difficult situation, with you coming on strong,' she said resentfully. 'I didn't want to lose the job—so I was trying to evade your attentions without hurting your ego.'

He gave a snort of disbelief. 'How very considerate of you! I could almost believe your story. You plead your cause well.'

Mariann's mouth compressed with exasperation. 'It's not a cause!' she cried indignantly. 'You've got to believe me! For the last time, I'm trying to tell you that we got off on the wrong foot—and why.'

'Hmm. I'm not sure. I'm rarely wrong about women,' he said thoughtfully.

'You are this time!' she retorted.

'We'll see.' He paused, frowning. 'You really want me to leave the bathroom? You don't want me to make love to you?'

'I don't,' she said, her eyes solemn and anxious. 'I just want to clean this stuff off my legs.' And then she could ask to brush her hair in his bedroom and perhaps find those keys. 'Please, don't be offended; I'd say the same to any man who made that suggestion.'

'Well, I am surprised. I was getting entirely different messages. Your body language is confusing.'

His eyebrow lifted when she jerked back after finding herself earnestly leaning towards him. And when she closed her parted lips and put her hand to her mouth, she knew he'd logged that down too as evidence of her guilt.

'I am confused, that's why,' she muttered.

'If I've misjudged you, I apologise. And I will make amends. However, if you're playing a clever, double deception, then God help you!' His gaze dropped to her orange legs. 'Get those stains off,' he ordered. 'When you've finished, I'll have decided what to do with you.'

'Yes, sir,' she said with mock-submission, irritated that she dared not object to being bossed around. Keeping him sweet was too important, but being meek to a tyrant was a bitter pill!

'No more playing a part, please,' the tyrant said sardonically. 'You're not the humble type and probably never were. As I said before, you're a woman who knows what she wants and how to get it.' A wintry smile cracked his stony face. 'I wonder if you will?'

She was filled with an urge to hurl a potted plant at him. 'I want to get the stain off my legs,' she said with grim conviction. And then get his keys. And run, she added to herself.

'It looks as though I'll be begging your forgiveness when you emerge, for accusing you of attempted deception,' he said evenly, and then strolled out, closing the door behind him. It opened again. His face appeared, dark, harsh, the scar livid on his cheekbone. 'Unless I find evidence to the contrary in the meantime,' he said softly. 'In which case, prepare yourself for a living hell.'

Totally drained, Mariann collapsed against a Baroque marble table, shaking from head to foot. What did he mean, finding evidence to the contrary? She racked her brains but couldn't see how he could do that. If he rang Antal, he'd get corroboration of her story. He wouldn't be able to contact the decorators till the morning. There was no one else who could endanger her mission—though she'd need to complete it before dawn.

Hopefully, he was just being his usual tyrannical, bullying self! She released all her tightly held breath in a long, satisfying growl of fury. It felt as though he'd turned her inside out and put her on a line to dry!

What a man. Lionel had mentioned Vigadó's fanatical attention to detail, his methodical care, and a tendency to hang on hard to something, like a dog worrying a bone, till he'd extracted everything he wanted. But, far from Vigadó resembling—as Lionel had claimed—a resolutely trundling tank that slowly and surely obliterated everything in its path, the brute was mentally alert and unnervingly sharp. Vigadó's mind moved with the speed of light and was just as illuminating. 'Back on guard,' she told herself ruefully. 'This one's going to be one heck of a challenge!'

Now what? She examined her legs. The stain seemed worse. But a bath seemed risky. Trembling at her narrow escape from Vigadó's bed, she wasn't prepared to tempt fate by stripping off in his bathroom. Yet...there *was* a hefty bolt on the door. She put her ear to the yellowing magnolia woodwork and heard him moving around, the sound of Hungarian music, the slam of a wardrobe door, the 'ting' of a telephone being picked up.

Taking a chance, she slid the bolt across and turned the big brass key for good measure. Fine. He couldn't get at her now! She'd weathered the teeth of the gale; her chances of coming through the rest of the storm were high. He'd finally conceded that she might be on the level and that was promising.

Feeling her pulse-rate slowly returning to normal, she whipped off her clothes and stepped into the breast-high water. 'Wonderful!' she murmured, allowing herself a giggle of relief at being free of Vigadó's oppressive threats.

Quietly she began to hum a tune. This was sheer luxury! A fabulous wallow in the kind of bathroom she'd always dreamed of. There were panelled walls, a stucco ceiling—admittedly flaking and badly in need of decoration, but with a chandelier!—marble floor, antique furniture everywhere.

Mariann stretched out in the enormous bath and let her body float to the surface, thinking out her strategy. It must be a complete, total denial of any ulterior motives. And a solemn, dogged insistence that her one aim in life at the moment was to decorate his office. Then she'd divert his attention, rifle through his pockets, and get the first plane home. She shivered at the thought of his revenge if he ever found out why she had really come to Budapest.

Glaring at her pinkish marmalade legs, she considered the consequences should she fail. Her face grew still. Her boss was so screwed up that he might well do something dramatic. She'd never seen a man driven so close to the edge before—not even her father, who'd grieved inconsolably when her mother had died. And Lionel's misery was Vigadó's fault entirely. He was a terrible man, she thought grimly, deserving the very worst!

With an angry inhalation, Mariann pushed herself upright again and began to scrub her shins ferociously. Her own job was on the line, too, of course, and just when she'd achieved her ambition to be an editor she was being threatened with redundancy. All the time she'd been an editor's secretary and had read the occasional manuscript, she'd known without vanity that she had a flair for the work. Her interview with Lionel had been brief and conclusive. He'd said she had 'prospects'. And she wasn't going to let her hard work and hours of dedication be set back by the likes of Vigadó Gabór.

Surveying her efforts gloomily, she stood up. The water whooshed down her legs as she fiercely soaped her paint-spattered thighs. Now the prospects had lost their promise. If only Mary hadn't accepted Vigadó's Monopoly-money offer!

'Swine!' she muttered.

'Language.'

Horrified, she jerked her head around. In a curtained alcove that she realised must lead from the bedroom stood Vigadó. And the malevolence in his face hit her like a blow to the stomach.

'Oh, God!' she breathed. Instinctively her arms crossed over and her hands went to cover her womanhood but she was so astonished that she did nothing else, only gaped at him, rooted to the spot, the water chilling on her body. 'What do you want?' she croaked, choking with fury and fear.

His eyes glittered with hostility. 'Guess.'

Mariann went white. She was naked, standing up in a bath, a few feet separating them and no suitable weapon to hand. It looked as though it had come down to a choice between keeping Vigadó happy and getting those darn keys, or keeping her virginity and rejecting his advances. No contest. Goodbye job, she thought morosely, consumed with an angry dismay.

'Is this the pounce? The classic bath scene?' she grated, her eyes flashing emerald lights.

'Depends.'

'I'm not interested,' she snapped, jerking up her chin haughtily. 'Would you leave?'

'My own bathroom?' he mocked. 'Why the hell should I?'

'A gentleman——!' she began hotly.

'You surely don't imagine for one split-second that I am a gentleman, do you?' he jeered. With leisurely movements, he folded his arms, making no attempt to disguise his slow, sensual judgement of her glistening body.

Her eyes flicked to the towel, at too great a distance for her to grab. 'Get out!' she yelled. He didn't stir a muscle and she silently seethed. 'This is intolerable! You can't treat me with contempt just because I'm a working girl!' she grated, amazed that fire and flames weren't coming out of her mouth.

'No,' he admitted softly. 'But I could if I discovered that you were persistently and deliberately deceiving me. And I did warn you. I gave you a chance to realise what kind of enemy I'd make and to take the sensible way out: a quick exit. You chose to plough on. I don't know whether to admire or despise you.'

Her spine became rigid with tension. 'Deceiving you?' she repeated faintly. Mariann was appalled. What had he based that on? What had she said? 'Look, please,' she begged hoarsely, 'let me dress and we'll talk. I can explain. I'm at something of a disadvantage here——'

'That's right,' he said with grim satisfaction.

Her mouth dropped open. 'You bastard!' she breathed.

'Oh, yes. Every single inch of me,' he growled. And she realised that there was an intense, ungovernable anger simmering away inside him. 'I'm of the opinion—correct me if I'm wrong—that you'll be more inclined to confess your sins if I keep you standing there,' he snarled. 'It's difficult to maintain any sense of dignity or superiority when stark naked, isn't it?'

'Monster!' she accused in dismay. 'I'm getting c-cold!'

'You could get even colder,' he said heartlessly. 'And if you don't tell me exactly what you're doing here in the next five seconds, then you'll find yourself—a few hours from now—outside in the snow. Very shocked. Very bruised. *Very* naked.' His dark eyes flashed with cruel silver.

'Did you say...*hours* from now?' she whispered.

'My vengeance would take time,' he said softly. 'I imagine that in your job you may have been roughed up or even abused by men before but I'm a master at domination. You see, I'm not burdened with pity.'

Her breathing rasped through her parted lips. For a few seconds it was all she could do, her whole body frozen with terror. 'I—you couldn't—you wouldn't dare!' she squeaked.

'I would,' he said with soft menace. 'I could. My muscles have been hardened in the best gyms in the world. More to the point, my heart has been hardened by some of the most beautiful women in the world. As for daring...' He gave an expressive shrug. 'I've raided more companies and sacked more staff than you've had hot dinners.'

He'd dare. No doubt about that. She gritted her teeth and tried not to shiver. 'Touch me and I'd tell! The scandal——'

'It's common knowledge that women chase me,' he said icily. 'Friends have even been with me when I've walked into my hotel room and found naked women in my bed.' His mouth curled down in contempt at her rounded eyes. 'Yes. People who've tried to create scandals have failed up to now because there's been no irrefutable evidence. I could say the same thing happened this time. A whore on the make. With previous attempts to blackmail me on record, I'd have no trouble shrugging off any accusations you chose to make.'

Mariann's mouth gaped. He thought she was a gold-digging hooker! Mercifully, he'd got the wrong end of the stick! Now all she had to do was to convince him he was wrong. 'Why do you think I'm deceiving you? What sins do you think I'm guilty of?' she asked hoarsely. 'Why suddenly think that I——?'

'I went through your bag,' he informed her coldly.

'You *what*? How *dare* you?' she spluttered. 'There's nothing in there to in——'

'Exactly,' he bit.

'Pardon?' Mariann said, bewildered.

'Nothing to incriminate you,' he said softly. 'That's what I find strange. And highly suspicious.' She trembled, nausea rising in her throat at the fury in his eyes. 'Your bag is full of the usual junk women cart around with them. Plus chocolates, string, maps, postcards, glue, sewing kit, pocket torch——'

'So?' she asked, attempting to be haughty.

Vigadó leant against the wall, a mocking smile faintly touching his lips. 'You're remarkably prepared for any event short of a typhoon,' he observed in glacial tones.

'Efficiency and foresight aren't whipping offences!' she defended. And he smiled menacingly as though he thought they might be. When did he ever *stop*? she wailed inside. He went on and on, grinding away, relentlessly pursuing every avenue, exhausting her.

'There was nothing to identify you,' he said calmly. 'No passport, credit cards, business cards, driving licence, diary or letters. Now *that's* suspicious.'

Mariann cringed back. 'No,' she moaned weakly.

'I knew you were lying!' he grated. 'Right from the start I was suspicious. I kept pushing you, testing you and you kept proclaiming your innocence. But then, when I mentioned sex, you backed off like a frightened virgin. And you did that so well that I thought I must have made a mistake and so I eased off. But it was only a ploy to put me off the scent, wasn't it? You're very clever! Too damn clever!'

'And you're wrong!' she breathed.

'Not about the phone number you carelessly left in your purse,' he said with soft savagery.

'Phone . . . ?' She licked her lips. Lionel had said he'd be going away and had left a contact number. It was scribbled on a small scrap of paper that only a Sherlock Holmes would find. She'd taken every other precaution! How *could* he have found it? Yet . . . surely if Vigadó had tried the number Lionel would have answered with his usual curt, Yes? Nothing incriminating about that——

'I rang the number,' Vigadó said in a conversational tone. 'It was a local railway station.' His eyes flickered at the way her body visibly relaxed in relief. 'I then dialled England.' The barely contained violence lit his face with a ruthlessness that made her skin crawl. 'And,' he said huskily, 'as you say—bingo!'

'You got through?' she croaked.

His index finger ran menacingly down the line of his scar. 'To a call-girl agency. I pretended to be a dirty old man in a mac and they offered me a range of women from blonde to bald and all the permutations in between.'

'But...!' It was incredible. The coincidence was too cruel, too unlikely... 'That can't be right!' she wailed. 'You rang the wrong number; you made a mistake——'

'Shut up! I made no mistake!'

'The wrong connection——'

'*There is no mistake*!' Shaking with anger, he flung her a towel. 'Get out of there before I drag you out!' he snarled.

With fumbling fingers, she tucked the towel around her. Lionel, she thought frantically. Perhaps he'd given her the wrong number! But would he use a place like that himself? She could hardly stop herself shaking. Life was throwing everything it had at her and she wanted *out*.

'Now what?' she husked nervously.

'Now you sing for your supper,' he grated.

'I'll sing at your funeral first!' she said wildly.

'Let me correct that, so my meaning is clear. You're going to crawl for your supper!' He came slowly towards her. 'Crawl to me.' His eyes flashed a dark desire. 'With me.' His mouth arched sensually. 'On me,' he whispered greedily. 'Beneath me!'

Mariann screamed. Nothing came out. Her breasts heaved rapidly beneath her protective arms. 'You can't mean that!' she mouthed in silent anguish.

'I mean it! You'll do whatever I want, wherever I want, however I want!' he lashed, still coming, his eyes blisteringly angry. 'And as often as I want!'

Petrified out of her life, Mariann took a step back and slipped on the soap. As she went down, her back connected with the rim of the bath, briefly knocking her breath from her body, and she slid under the deep water so fast that she didn't even have time to grab the sides.

Vigadó's strong arms hauled her out with rough force, lifting her up coughing and spluttering, while a wail of fear struggled upwards from the depths of her body. Suspended just above the water, entirely at his mercy, she groaned and blindly sank her teeth into the thick seam of his jacket.

'Nnn!' she grated, rigid with terror.

'You little fool!' he barked. 'Hang on to my neck. I'll lift you out.'

'Nnn!'

'Ready?' he muttered roughly.

Mercifully gentle, he raised her, still wrapped in the saturated towel that must have soaked him to the skin in seconds. But she didn't care. She could think of nothing but her anger.

He placed her on the thick bathmat as though, she thought hysterically, he were laying out a dead butterfly in a case. One he'd caught and was about to pin out for his collection!

'Ohh!' she groaned in despair. Still hovering over her, he slicked excess water from her face and hair with his fingers.

'You do seem to have taken a dislike to my suits, don't you?' he said in exasperation.

'Your *suits*?' she choked in fury. She hated *him*! A flash of muscle pain stopped her from telling him so and for a moment she clenched her jaw tightly, waiting for the spasm to go away.

'Try not to tense up,' he advised curtly.

'I am trying! It's difficult—with you—threatening my—virginity,' she rasped.

'Your what?' he scathed. 'God! You do have a talent for the ridiculous! Listen. I'm going to move you to the bedroom in a moment——'

'No!' she squeaked. Oh, God! she thought. He was going to go through with his threat!

He growled under his breath. 'You've got to release that pain or your muscles will seize up and go into spasm. I've seen this kind of injury before——'

'Frightened women—in the bath—all over—Hungary?' she muttered breathily.

'My father,' he said with a dark scowl. 'Don't fight it. Get your breathing as regular as you can.'

He was right; she'd tightened everything in her body that moved. So she tried to breathe more deeply and relax. 'Can't,' she said tersely, her imploring eyes on his. 'Can't!'

'Yes, you damn well can. You're the kind who can do anything. Including, it seems, deliberately launching yourself into space and also attempting to drown yourself to divert my sympathies. Well, I haven't got any.'

Ruthless brute! 'Both were accidents!' she whispered.

'Unlikely, in the circumstances,' he growled.

She closed her eyes in exasperation and then, for a moment, it felt as though his mouth had touched her temple. She wanted to check, but was too nervous because his hand had begun to stroke her forehead. It swept around her face, her jawline, her bare neck.

'Relax, relax,' he coaxed, his voice low and husky, the accent thickening and lacing the words with sensuality. His fingers slid away and began to smooth up and down her leg in a slow, hypnotic rhythm that was causing her to melt into the floor.

'Vigadó!' she croaked, unjamming her teeth and slowly opening her eyes and meeting his, hot, dark, savage man-wants-woman eyes. Meltdown temperature hit her loins, one of the few parts that didn't hurt. Her arms seemed to be wound around his neck.

And then she remembered the kind of man he was and that he was married.

Heaven help her terrible weakness for him! She blinked at the shameful knowledge of what she wanted to do next, her mouth pouting with resentment at her flagrant lack of sense. A kiss, she thought dizzily. That would be...

'Relaxing?' He must have recognised her confusion because he read the message of her lips and kissed her, lightly, brushing his lips across hers, arousing all the sensitive nerves around her mouth till they were screaming through her body.

No kiss had done that to her before. If she hadn't been injured, she feared that she might have liquefied in his arms and deepened the embrace, sighed, moaned, wriggled against him. She was hungry. Oh, God! She was hungry! Trembling, she tried to gather her scattered senses and put her sinful lapse of standards down to feeling light-headed.

'I can't—breathe properly!' she whispered.

Her mouth was closed by his, tenderly exploring, softening all her muscles and warming her through and through. 'That's better,' he husked in smug approval, and she raged inside that she'd fallen for his tactics. No wonder he had a big head, she thought sullenly, if he had the same effect on every female in sight. 'Now I suppose I ought to unwrap the towel and check you over.'

'You can't do that!' she gasped.

He frowned. 'You've tensed up again.'

'You bet!' she croaked.

Again, he let his lips roam her flushed face while she protested weakly, torn between the pleasure of his caresses and the need to free herself. This was an opportunist of the first order! She was feeble and at his mercy. So he took advantage. Brute!

'You must relax.' He frowned. 'Breathe out——'

'I don't trust you,' she muttered.

'You're showing some sense at last,' he said sardonically. 'But there isn't much you can do to stop me from doing whatever I want, is there?'

'You *devil*!' she wailed, frantically avoiding his swooping mouth and knowing with a mortifying misery that part of her anger was due to the fact that she'd wanted his kisses with an urgent, overwhelming passion she'd never felt before. Filled with anger and pain she might be, but she could willingly sink into those brawny gold arms and while the rest of the evening away and enjoy every second.

No, she reminded herself, in despair. He had a wife. Admitting to wanting him, however briefly, made her no better than the harlot he imagined her to be. A pain slashed through her heart.

'I hurt,' she said weakly, playing for sympathy.

'And I am totally, undeniably ruthless,' he snarled. 'If there's one thing that makes me blind with fury, it's when someone tries to make a fool of me. I'll make use of your weakness if I have to. I know your game and refuse to play it—in fact, you're going to play mine. Before you do, I want to know who hired you. I'll find out, the hard way or the easy way. It's your choice,' he said, his voice rising. 'I warn you that the stakes are high enough for me to be perfectly prepared to keep you here on the floor for a week, you little tramp!' he roared.

CHAPTER FOUR

MARIANN was appalled. 'I'm cold, wet, in pain,' she grated, exaggerating. Her chest hardly hurt now. 'You can't be so inhuman——'

'The bathroom's centrally heated, and you feel warm to me,' he said cynically. 'And besides, you could be warmer, dry and cosseted by the best doctor in Budapest,' he growled. 'Just tell me what I want to know; who hired you to seduce me and compromise my position at Dieter Ringel?'

She blinked. Was that what he imagined? 'Who *what*? Are you serious?' she said huskily.

'My commercial enemies will do anything,' he muttered through clenched teeth. 'Publishing is a dog-eat-dog business. It's not the first time this has been tried, nor will it be the last. I've made a lot of enemies on the way up. They believe I can only be brought to my downfall by my sexual misjudgement. This, so I've been informed, is my Archilles' heel.'

'Women?' she said, not hiding her disdain.

He touched the scar thoughtfully. 'Sure. The rest of my life is watertight and unassailable,' he drawled. 'I find the methods of my enemies irritating, however unsuccessful they always turn out to be. They have this fixed idea of me...so they keep trying. When I get my hands on them...' His expanded chest and blazing eyes told her that the result wouldn't be pretty. She shuddered. 'Are you going to tell me who they are and what they're paying you?' he demanded.

'Of course not! I——'

'Damn you!' he roared. 'You're stupid beyond belief to remain loyal to a bunch of people who can't get anywhere on their own merits, but have to lie and cheat instead,' he added savagely.

'Why should I be part of some melodramatic plot to——? Oh, God, this is too ridiculous!' she snapped. 'I'm supposed to be trying to seduce *you*? You said everyone knew how women throw themselves at your feet ten times a minute——'

'But this is different,' he said silkily. 'You are different. Quite a class act. Those who really know me never took those gold-digging women seriously. I can deal with cheaply hired tramps and even would-be mistresses without raising a sweat. However, this is far more dangerous an operation. You've taken trouble to set up an innocent cover, and have even begun to paint my office. Someone must have helped you set all that up. We're talking about bigger stakes here than a woman on the make and I want to know exactly what they are.'

'We are?' she said nervously. 'You do?'

'Oh, yes. I can recognise guilt when I see it!' he growled. 'You're involved somehow in a multi-million-dollar scam. I'm aware that there's a campaign to get me removed from Dieter Ringel. But you're only wasting your time. The attempt has fallen flat because I'm too firmly entrenched now. I have very carefully made myself indispensable. And nothing, *nothing* will make me give up what I've fought for, what I've sacrificed the whole of my life for! Now, who hired you?' he demanded, thrusting his face within inches of hers. 'Who?'

'My God, you know some awful people!' she muttered—and yelped as he angrily flung open the sodden, heavy folds of the towel to expose her naked breasts. When her hands flew to cover herself he caught them roughly and they wrestled in grim silence for a moment, their eyes clashing in battle till he overpowered her. 'You bastard, you bastard!' she whispered, furious to be defeated. 'I need a doctor!' she lied in desperation.

'I don't think you do. But you might need surgery,' he said savagely, 'by the time I've finished with you!'

Terrified, Mariann let the tears show in her eyes. 'Help me!' she whispered.

'You'll get help when you've confessed all.' Despite his angry tone, he was running his free hand lightly over her ribs beneath her breasts as though making sure she was all right. 'However, I'm prepared to see how badly you were injured. Not as seriously as you're making out, I think.' He was unmoved by her plight, unmoved, it seemed, by her nakedness.

'Ow!' she said sullenly at the pressure of his fingers. And she felt deeply humiliated. Judging by the constant burning heat that flowed to her very core, her skin must be scarlet! Close to tears of shame, she wriggled, pressing her thighs tightly together.

'Is there pain anywhere else?' he asked callously.

'Everywhere!' She sniffed, exaggerating her internal ache. 'No!' she corrected with a squeal of panic. 'Don't touch me anywhere else!'

A frown creased the broad, tanned brow. 'Embarrassed?' His indifferent gaze swept down the whole length of her body and Mariann closed her eyes tightly as though that would make her invisible. Suddenly his accusing eyes were on hers again. 'You're distracting me by acting coy!' he snapped.

'And you're deliberately degrading me!' she jerked.

'Yes.'

She swallowed miserably. 'Please cover me up,' she intoned.

'When I have the information I want,' he answered with an implacable expression. 'Besides, I enjoy beauty and I can amuse myself with studying your lovely body while I wait for you to answer. Study, and touch... Flawless skin,' he mused, touching her hip.

Her pelvic muscles contracted, drawing his eyes, which glazed over in an unnervingly drowsy way, his finger tracing patterns on her hipbone that branded her with heat and sent heated blood around her increasingly feverish body.

'Don't!' she husked.

'You're for sale. And I buy beautiful artefacts, Mimi. Mimi!' he scorned, jerking his hand away as though angry with himself. 'For God's sake, what kind of name is that? Do you think I'm an innocent child? This is all a joke to you, isn't it?'

'No!' she wailed. He'd returned his attention to her ribcage and the warmth of his big, capable hands spread over her chest as he sternly tested her reaction to the tentative, inching pressure of his sensitive thumbs. His palm hesitated on her erratically pumping heart and his eyes shot up to search hers with a puzzled expression in them. 'You don't understand!' she cried. And in sheer frustration and pain she burst into tears. 'It isn't a joke to me at all!'

'So you admit it,' he grated. 'This is a professional job you're doing.'

'Oh, help! I need a moment to think. Leave me *alone*, will you!' Mariann bit her lower lip to control her sobs.

'A woman's tears don't move me at all,' he said softly.

'I never imagined they would!' she countered defiantly.

She was trapped. If she denied his accusation that she was a call-girl who'd been hired to compromise him, then he'd want to probe further and she didn't have any reserves of strength left to fight his interrogation. All she wanted was to be warm, to curl up in a soft bed and sleep. She trembled at the thought of the potential violence stored in that big, threatening body looming over her.

It seemed that her loss of personal dignity had knocked her sideways. She'd always been in control before; losing it so utterly had left her shaken and vulnerable. Or...was it the fact that he'd burnt into her sleeping sexual subconscious and woken it, with devastating consequences? It hardly mattered. Whatever she said, however much she denied his accusations, her prospects of acquiring the keys in the way she'd planned were receding all the time.

Perhaps the only solution was to let him think whatever he wanted and save herself any more hassle. She'd have to go back to England and admit defeat. And yet the thought of what her failure would do to Lionel made her want to weep. He'd had a raw deal, poor man. If only she could have eased his misery! Somehow she would, she vowed. Somehow. Surely she had the wit to cook up another scheme!

'I know nothing of this attempt to compromise you,' she muttered.

'Liar!' he grated.

'I swear! I swear by all that's holy to me!'

'Your looks?' he scathed. 'My, that's pretty convincing!'

'You swine!' she rasped through her teeth. 'I—I was just told by the boss of my firm to do this job,' she cried desperately, her conscience preventing her from a direct lie. 'He told me little else! You've got to believe me!'

'Who approached him? Who paid?' he insisted roughly.

'I don't know anything about that,' she answered evasively. 'He told me the name of the company and where it was and he told me a little about you. I suppose there was no reason to tell me any more than I had to know. That's the truth!'

'Damn! I need to know——'

'Why?' she wailed. 'What difference does it make?'

'The difference,' he said tightly, 'is that I'd be able to take a very unpleasant revenge. I suppose you wouldn't be told,' he muttered to himself. He frowned and reached for a dry towel. Draping it carefully around her, he saw that she flinched warily from his touch and obviously thought it was from pain. 'Easy. Easy.'

'I'm not a horse,' she muttered.

'Women and horses,' he growled, 'need a firm hand.' She glared up at the arrogant set of his head, only to be electrified by the sensuous lines of his mouth. Two dark, turbulent eyes captured hers and her flesh shimmered with the tremor that ran through her. A caressing hand lightly cupped her face but the set of his jaw was like steel. 'Man must ride the horse,' he husked. 'Not the horse the man.'

He was a pagan. Caveman personified, the animal sexuality driving his passions, sweeping away any decency and replacing it with a carnal hunger that had to be satisfied, no matter what the cost. And in her weakness she was unable to hold back her own primitive response to his intense, impassioned eyes, the low huskiness of his voice, his rough, compelling command. Vigadó was man at his most basic: hunt, see, kill or capture. For some mortifying reason, she found that wildly exciting.

'Please,' she said, her voice slurred and unrecognisable.

'I might. We'll get to that later,' he breathed in a sexy, sense-scattering growl.

Afraid of what was to come, she groaned out loud. It sounded horribly like a moan of need. And he stroked her forehead with feathering fingers, watching her...watching, watching.

Oh, God! she thought, making her eyes glaze over. Mariann felt bewildered by what was happening to her. His threat had sent waves of indolent pleasure coursing through all her veins. Had she been unmoved by other men because none of them was forceful enough? She'd gone weak at the knees the moment he'd turned on his ferocious battering-ram technique.

Why this man, of all others? she wailed silently. Her head was spinning. Of course! she decided, clutching any straw to hand. Her hysteria was due to the fall she'd had. It must be that.

She'd been brought up with strict Victorian morals. Sex was for husband and wife. It hadn't been hard to stay a virgin. Nobody had ever made her feel intoxicated by touching her before, by gazing at her as though she was the most exciting woman in the world, by threatening her, and yet... Her eyes widened. And yet sounding as though he was desperate—yes, desperate—to possess her!

Something had gone wrong with her antennae. He loathed her, felt contempt and was intending to use her. Mariann's huge, darkened eyes searched his and she let out a small whimper. She saw an inexplicable tenderness, and it made her heart contract.

His hand slid down her face. One finger reached out, mesmerising her as it came closer and closer and then came into contact with the bow of her wide mouth. Automatically her lips parted for him—in fear, she hastily told herself—as she gasped in a little shaky breath. The black fringe of his lashes fluttered on the Slavonic cheekbones and he gave a small smile that weakened the whole of her body.

'You're the most beautiful woman I've ever seen.'

Stark. Corny. But spoken in those harsh, accented tones, with a dark and thrilling undercurrent of barely controlled passion, it created a soaring, delighted pride inside her and intensified the emptiness of her body.

Mariann turned her head to one side and ruthlessly fixed her gaze on the far wall, forcing her pulses to stop thudding with such humiliating urgency. Was she *crazy*? No wonder women fell like ninepins, faced with Vigadó's sheer animal magnetism. There was sex in the very bones of his body. He was the archetypal male and, unfortunately for her, she'd been programmed by wanton genes to desire him.

Escape. She had to. Or...

'I've failed in my job.' Mariann frowned and cleared her throat. Horrifyingly, she felt a reluctance to leave. But then, her father had always said that the devil was Mr Fascination himself. She turned her head to one side to avoid his terrible, glittering eyes. 'I won't bother you any more. You know everything now. Let me go,' she said tonelessly.

There came the rustle of cloth and she jerked her head back in alarm. With panic-stricken eyes she watched him slide off his saturated jacket and let it flop soggily to the floor. Then he stripped off his shirt faster than she could have believed possible to reveal an expanse, of taut, dark skin over his chest which was struggling to contain powerfully developed muscles. Stunning. He was...beautiful. Her breath shuddered in raggedly and a knifing stab of desire told her that she wouldn't stand a chance against his advances.

'Why are you...?' She licked parched lips and the mocking light in his eyes lashed her with brutal male contempt. It was obvious. Her punishment. 'No! Oh, don't!' she moaned through stiff lips. And sought his mercy. 'Can't you see what a state I'm in?'

'Yes,' he grated, his teeth bared as if he wanted to devour her then and there. 'Excited.'

Oh, you brute, Mariann intoned inwardly. You brute. In the ensuing silence, she suddenly felt cheap and soiled and frightened. 'You'll hurt me!' she croaked in horror. 'It'll be no fun; you'll—you'll hate it! I'll—I'll sue you for every penny you've got; I'll—oh, please, I don't want to be hurt——'

He grunted, lifting her up and carrying her feebly struggling body through the curtained alcove.

'Hurt?' he murmured. 'A woman like you?'

'You can't be stupid enough to do this,' she moaned as he walked into his brothel-house bedroom, all red silk and purple satins, to the high four-poster. 'Please, you can't——'

'You must know some bastards,' he said grimly, placing her with surprising gentleness on the soft mattress.

'I do,' she muttered. Him.

He was tucking her under the duvet. She lay in terror, waiting, ready to scream, but there was no one around to hear her cries. No one at all. Staring around the room like a hunted animal, she saw something familiar. The silver frame of his wife's photograph, face-down on the chest of drawers. She gave a sob of anger at her weak condition and cursed herself for ever being tempted by evil.

'Now I'll tell you what I'm going to do,' he said softly.

She put her hands over her ears, expecting to hear a recitation of the spicier parts of the *Kama Sutra*. 'No,' she husked. 'No!'

Without gentleness, he pulled her hands away, quite unmoved by her petrified face. 'What *do* you expect?' he growled. 'What have men done to you before, that you should show such fear now?'

'I've heard . . . things about you,' she said lamely. And she blushed, remembering how she'd stopped Lionel telling her with relish how Vigadó had brutalised his own wife with outlandish bedroom demands. She shuddered. She'd never imagined that she'd be subjected to those same demands. Or more inventive ones. 'Let me go!' she said fiercely.

'I will. Contrary to what your experience—or your imagination—is telling you to expect from me, I mean to let you rest here till you feel well enough to leave——'

'Leave?' She almost choked in her haste to be sure she'd heard aright. 'You mean it?'

'I mean it.'

'Now! I can go now!' So desperately relieved to be reprieved, Mariann didn't question his decision but sat up hastily, dragging the duvet with her. And she saw something that she'd missed before—his discarded charcoal suit, draped on a low chair. Her eyes widened. She could get the keys. Even now. Somehow.

'I insist that you stay, to make sure you're all right. A short time,' he said softly.

'Very short,' she said, trying to sound reluctant.

He smiled. 'I thought you might.'

'And then——'

'I'm going to be paying you at some time in the near future,' he said calmly. 'For my gratitude in releasing me from hell. For services rendered.'

Mariann froze, wondering what that hell might be but knowing only that 'services rendered' probably had sexual connotations. Then she called his bluff. 'For clearing the room, undercoating, emulsioning the ceiling——'

'For something else, much more basic to my needs. But first, tell me are you almost recovered now?'

'Almost,' she replied nervously and jumped when the telephone jangled close to her ear.

Smiling, he sat on the bed and reached across her. 'Excuse me,' he murmured. For a few moments, he listened as a man's voice crackled on the other end of the line. His body tensed noticeably. He asked the man to wait a moment and then his glance flicked to the top of the chest of drawers and back to Mariann. '*Talán ... jó. Kösönöm szépen,*' he said, wavering over some decision and then giving the go-ahead with a quiet thank-you.

He replaced the receiver. 'At last,' he said under his breath. 'And earlier than I'd planned.' And then his hands came to rest on either side of her body, making her a prisoner in the bed. 'The faithful janitor,' he explained. 'And now,' he said, with bloodthirsty relish, 'we make love.'

'You cheat!' she yelled. A surge of fury enabled her to whisk out her arms from beneath the bedding and thrust hard against his shoulders to halt the menacing body. He rocked with the force of her movement but kept coming. 'I'll scream!' she croaked.

'Then I fear I must be a little rougher,' he husked, capturing her hands.

He spread her arms to each side, his naked torso an inch from hers. His face swam before her alarmed eyes, the fear making her pant sharply at the knowledge that she had no defence against him now.

'Leave me alone!' she whispered.

'Stop fighting! You were going to coax me to make love to you anyway,' he reasoned silkily. 'Does it matter that I'm in charge instead of you? This won't take long and I will be careful not to injure you. All I ask is that you lie there and don't struggle.' His voice thickened and he licked his lips as though they were dry from the parching heat of his hot breath. 'Not much to ask, is it?'

'Not . . . I—you're talking rape!' gasped Mariann, her face bloodless. 'I knew you were violent! You get your kicks out of raping women—dominating in the most demeaning way!'

His eyes blazed. 'I only want to use you as——!'

'*Use* me?' she cried hoarsely. 'Is that all? Words fail me! You low-down——!'

'Submit,' he murmured. 'What is it to you? You'll get paid well.'

Her mistake was to open her mouth to protest. For a moment she sought to avoid the pressure of his mouth on hers, the terror of his invasion of her body so fierce that she was fired with an unholy strength.

But slowly, inexorably, his kiss told her body something different. Her mind cried, 'Rape, violence, brutality,' but her heart, emotions, the very core of her being was yielding to sweet—oh, infinitely sweet!—seduction. It was so impassioned and prolonged a kiss, so desperate and hungry, that it destroyed her will. She felt like that too. Without knowing, she'd wanted a man to break down her self-imposed barriers and sweep her off her feet. But not a man like this! she thought in despair. Everything was wrong about him...

Almost everything. Incapable of escaping, nevertheless she struggled because to be acquiescent would give him the wrong impression—and because she would have despised herself for not resisting.

But long and deep and slow, the kiss and her confused brain combined to obliterate everything from her mind and her body softened despite her intentions, her hands sliding over the beautiful, firm skin, along the sloping muscles of his shoulders to lodge at the nape of his neck. Somehow he'd pulled back the duvet and her breasts were brushing his chest, each soft peak tightening in a wonderful agony and throbbing with an urgent beat.

Awash with a velvet warmth that enveloped her body, she tried to open her eyes but they kept closing in bliss. 'Vigadó!' she muttered helplessly in a desperate protest.

His hand moved to her throat, fondling its taut curves, stroking the frantic pulses then moving to the firm bone of her jaw. 'Beautiful,' he said hoarsely. 'Captivating. Special... Oh, God! You're exciting!'

Mariann tried to think straight. It was almost impossible to do so. Vigadó's mouth was gently, sweetly coaxing every inch of her lips into responding to his butterfly kisses, his hands now lightly moving down her arms... to her shoulders, her collarbone, the first swell of her breasts. And she could hardly breathe, her mind fighting her body, struggling to deny her terrible, wanton needs.

Treachery! she accused her senses.

Clutching a handful of his hair, she drew his head back with all her might and forced her emerald-flecked eyes open to glare at him.

His hands cupped her lushly curving breasts. Mariann felt her lower body contract while her breasts thrust with a humiliating eagerness deeper into his palms and she gave a pleasurable, horrified shudder when his thumbs flicked across each extended, pulsing nipple.

'Good?' he husked.

'Uh!' She barely stopped herself admitting it. Good? she thought dazedly as the intense pleasure fanned through her receptive body. It was unendurably exciting. This was why women were driven inexorably to share their bodies. Now she understood how desire could overcome sense, conscience, upbringing...

'I want you. So very, very badly,' he said raggedly.

His mouth possessed hers with a violent passion that left her clutching at him blindly, moaning into its dark warmth, wriggling beneath him and loving, hating the insistent ruthlessness of his stroking fingers, the indolent flicker of his searching tongue. Deeper and deeper she sank, trying to surface, trying to deny him, her body writhing sinuously, arching, rolling with him on the bed, sliding and slithering on the purple satin sheet, a wild tableau of naked arms and legs, her feet hooking around the soft material that stretched across his lean hips——

'My God! What's going on?'

The tableau froze. He, taut as a bowstring, that beautiful torso gleaming where the light bounced off the expanded muscles, an inexplicable mixture of smouldering hunger and strain on his face. She, totally naked, her pelvis against his, and even through the material of his trousers the hot thrust of his manhood pounding against her burning womanhood, pressing against the very place that tormented her with its ecstasy of carnal arousal.

'Good God! I forgot...!' he groaned, as though coming out of a dream.

Slowly, Mariann's horrified eyes slanted to the door. Vigadó slowly lifted his head as though it weighed heavily on his strong neck and turned to look over his shoulder. Gently he eased down her legs, his hand accidentally or intentionally caressing her neat buttocks as he did so.

'Oh, dear heaven!' she whispered feebly.

She saw a blonde woman, dainty, stony-faced, muffled up in white fox furs. The woman in the photograph. His wife? If Mariann could have hidden beneath the covers or leapt from the bed she would have done, but Vigadó's imprisoning hands kept her rigid.

'Eva!' he exclaimed hoarsely.

And, watched by the two open-mouthed women, he pushed a hand through his dishevelled hair and rolled to one side, totally exposing Mariann's naked body, the duvet so tangled up in his legs that when she reached for it to cover herself she ended up wrestling with it in vain and slowly turning a bright red as they both watched her frustrated efforts.

Eva, she thought miserably. Yes . . . his wife!

'What are you doing coming here, Eva?' he demanded, his voice thickened with frustrated passion.

What was she doing here? Mariann thought hysterically. Watching her husband apparently commit adultery, of course!

'Explain to her what happened!' she said furiously, holding a huge satin pillow in front of her. 'Tell her——'

'Bitch!' spat Eva, her mouth distorted in rage as she suddenly erupted into speech. 'You stupid woman! I suppose you think you've found a rich man for your lover? He can kiss goodbye to riches! We had an agreement,' she railed, glaring at the tense Vigadó. 'It's over. You are *finished*!'

'Tell her!' groaned Mariann. 'It wasn't my fault!' she grated. 'I refuse to take any responsibility——'

'No woman has come between us! But this . . . !' cried Eva distractedly.

'Why did you come, Eva?' he asked, almost gently.

'I heard you'd arrived. I thought I might...' Eva bit her lip. 'You promised!' she cried hysterically. 'No other women! I thought you couldn't——'

'*Eva!*' he snapped, his eyes blazing.

'You promised!' his wife sobbed. She made a small, throaty cry and ran out, slamming the front door behind her a few seconds later.

'Hell.' The word came from deep inside him, dredged up from the very depths of his body as though the scene had pained him as much as it had the two women. He detached himself from the distressed Mariann and stood up, a despair in his eyes, his forehead lined with strain. To her amazement, he was shaking. 'It's finished,' he repeated in a low, hoarse growl. 'It's all over.'

'My heart bleeds!' she raged shakily.

'Bitch.'

'I don't believe this! You're calling *me* names? You're only upset at losing your meal-ticket!' she snapped bitterly. 'You deserve it, you beast! I'm glad! You humiliated me!' Close to losing any control, she clutched the pillow with claw-like fingers to stop them trembling. 'You treated me—and your wife—without any thought to our feelings——'

'I'm sorry,' he said tightly. And sounded so.

Mariann stopped her planned torrent of abuse in surprise. Vigadó had his back to her but it was evident in every line of his body that he was going through some kind of private hell. 'You're *sorry*? I don't understand you! Everything you did then was deliberate... You knew someone was coming!' she accused. 'It's possible you knew that it was your wife—perhaps when the janitor rang you——'

He whirled around, his eyes dark with anguish. 'Yes, I knew! And then you wiped her from my mind, impossible though that sounds! And if you ever tell anyone I knew she was coming,' he said savagely, 'I will see that you regret every word you utter!'

Mariann flinched, her sensibilities shocked. 'What's going on?' she grated hoarsely. 'You did use me. But not in the way I thought you would!'

'You don't need to know anything,' he snarled. 'You're better out of it. Aren't you used to men using you for their own purposes?'

'My God!' she breathed.

'You were perfectly prepared to earn money in your usual way, by performing in my bed; at least this way you get paid without the effort of intercourse.' Mariann gasped. 'Oh, don't be so damned prim!' he said impatiently. 'What was that scene to you? A row between husband and wife. Nothing unusual. All the men you sleep with are cheating on someone, I imagine. You betray your own sex every day, don't you?'

'It was horrible,' she said shakily. And she wondered if she'd ever forget that woman's face, the skin stretched taut across her cheekbones, the horror in her eyes. She, Mariann, had been thrown into another world, one she'd never even imagined could exist. An underworld of pain and cruelty.

'You've served your purpose,' he said shortly. 'Now get dressed. I'll pay you. I've finished with you, thank God! And if it's any consolation, I loathe myself as much as I loathe you.'

Bewildered at his contemptuous dismissal of her, she watched him select a fresh shirt from the wardrobe.

'I've never known anyone as calculating or as inhuman as you!' she cried jerkily. The knowledge of what had happened was beginning to hit her. The shame, the degradation... Oh, Lionel! she thought miserably. I'm entangled in the lurid affairs of a married man! And what her father would think... 'I despise you!'

Her eyes filled with tears. She despised herself. That enticing feeling of indolence, of insane passion that she'd felt had been produced by a clever, scheming devil with no shame, no heart, and motivations too complex for her ever to understand.

'Not half as much as I despise myself,' he muttered quietly, unknowingly repeating the words she'd castigised herself with.

'I doubt it,' she seethed. 'That was a vile scene——'

'One I never want to repeat,' he said fiercely, his chest rising and falling heavily as though still on the brink of control. 'You've roused a part of me I'd thought long suppressed. And I can live better without it, you little witch!'

Her eyes grew big and frightened. Facing her was six feet one or so of raw muscle and bone, anger enough for the two of them and a mind ticking over the fact that unemployment might be in the offing for him when his wife reported back to her father.

'It wasn't my fault what happened! You deliberately threw yourself on me! I never wanted to hurt your wife!'

Vigadó was barely managing to regulate his breathing, let alone his temper. His teeth gleamed between his bared lips. Something had made him unreasonably angry. Unable to bear the intense lash of his eyes, she dropped her gaze—only to give a quick intake of breath at the hard outline distorting the once-perfect line of his trousers. Vigadó wanted her still—or, rather, he wanted sex. Very, very badly. She cringed.

'Yes. You *are* seeing my arousal. I could take you. No one would blame me,' he breathed.

'And despise yourself more?' she scorned shakily.

'The alternative is to suffer painful frustration.'

'Rubbish!' she husked. But she knew only too well what he might be feeling. So wound up was she that she wanted to thump the pillow, the wall—anything, him even. Her whole body felt cheated, her mind was confused and shocked. There had been a powerful build-up of energy between them. A gradual, inexorable arousal of physical craving that would need such reserves of stamina in its release that their bodies had, with pagan, animal knowing, instinctively gathered every scrap of vigour in preparation for the night ahead.

And now that energy had nowhere to go. He'd taken her to the edge of hell or heaven, she wasn't sure which, and her normally clear, incisive mind could hardly make sense of what was happening, only that she had a greater potential for uninhibited sex, for being the wanton, than she ever could have imagined in her wildest dreams.

'No. You know very well what fires we've lit between us, what you've done—are doing—to me,' he said thickly. 'You, of all women! My God! I should take you. For my own sanity, you little witch!'

'I am blameless!' she raged.

'No. You are woman.' His eyes melted and the core of her body liquefied as if he had set a torch to it. 'You are woman, I am man. It's as simple as that.'

CHAPTER FIVE

THE room seemed to spin. Mariann could hardly breathe. It was that simple. A primitive, thudding urgency pounded in her body. She was transfixed by his desire, electrified by his avid mouth, the slow, ruthless flow of his gaze over every tingling inch of her.

'Oh, dear heaven!' she mouthed. 'What kind of devil are you?'

'You say that?' he husked, his eyes glittering feverishly. 'You lie there—your whole body burning with desire, your mouth hungry for kisses, skin like honey, waiting with languorous ease to be ravished to exhaustion—and you call *me* a devil? If this were the Middle Ages, you'd be hanged for witchcraft!'

'No, no!' she denied, covering her face in shame and despair.

Her hands were dragged away. Vigadó's mouth was possessing hers, pushing her back to the pillow, his teeth grazing her jaw, his warm, sinuous tongue lightly sensitising the hollow of her cheek, the folds of her ear...

'Ohh!' she groaned.

And then he thrust her away, gave her a shake and stood brooding over her. 'You'd make a man forget everything he held dear,' he rasped. 'When men make love to you, they must find it impossible to return to their wives! You must ruin more marriages than you ever realise!' He drew a hand across his sweating brow. 'I don't know how you can live with your conscience. Don't you ever feel *dirty*, doing a job like this?' he growled.

Aghast at her hungry body, she lifted tearful eyes to his. 'Yes! I hate it!' she cried fiercely. She loathed the circumstances that had pushed her into such a tawdry situation. And which had brought her face to face with her own terrible sexuality. 'But you're as bad! You ought to feel dirty using me! You hypocrite!' she stormed almost hysterically.

'I had to use you!' he roared. 'My needs were greater than yours! Besides, you are already damned! It's all in a day's work to you! I can still get out of hell if I try hard enough. You've jumped in with both feet and obviously intend to stay there!'

'I had to do it!' she wailed.

'Had to? Your tune has changed. You seemed to find it amusing enough to start with,' he said grimly.

'I did my best to.' She sniffed miserably. 'The only way I can get through anything I don't like is to convince myself it's fun, to find something about the task I can enjoy or laugh about. Father told me there was something good in everything, and to find it, build on it. But that was before...' She closed her eyes to shut out the terrible memory of Vigadó's wife and found that she was shaking uncontrollably from the demeaning experience. Yes. She did feel dirty. Her flesh crawled. 'I can't stand being used!' she said huskily.

'It's over,' he said curtly. His mouth tightened as though he was in pain too. 'You won't be touched again. My pride wouldn't allow it.'

'I won't?' she breathed, lifting huge, tearful eyes to his.

'Disappointed?' he snapped.

'You must be joking!' she whispered. And she blanked out the rebellious thought that said she would regret for the rest of her life that she had not known his body.

His eyes glittered. 'I've had better compliments.'

'I've had better bathtimes,' she said bitterly.

He gave her a baleful glare. 'Your fault. If you hadn't lurched back——'

'Me?' she said furiously. '*Me*? How can you say that?'

'But you kept denying the truth. I was forced to teach you a lesson!' he grated.

'And then to use me,' she said in a low tone.

'Yes. That too,' he said grimly. 'If you're straight with me, I'll be straight with you. But I'll break any butterfly who tries to dazzle me with its pretty wings and leads me a dance.'

'I don't feel as if I'll ever fly again,' she grumbled.

'This might help lubricate the wings.' His whole body bristling with scorn, he peeled a thick pile of notes from his wallet and threw them on the bed.

She brushed them off defiantly. 'I don't want your money!' she yelled.

'Got enough from whoever hired you?' he snarled. 'Take what's offered you. It could be useful. Give you a rest from some of your more athletic ventures.'

'I feel sick,' she whispered.

He disappeared briefly. She breathed deeply and accepted a glass of water which he brought and thrust into her hand.

'That scene did disturb you,' he remarked curtly.

'Darn right it did,' she husked, her mouth tremulous.

Vigadó folded his arms across his barrel chest and let out a huge sigh. 'Why the hell do you make me feel guilty?' he muttered.

Mariann's eyes flashed up to his. 'Because you should,' she scowled. There was a silence while she finished the water and he studied her carefully, as though making up his mind about something. 'Don't even think it!' she warned mutinously.

'I have a proposition,' he said flatly.

'Forget it,' she snapped. 'All I want is my clothes. Please get them.'

'Work,' he said, continuing as though she'd never spoken. 'Honest, decent work. No sex. No deceptions. No jaded businessmen wanting a night of fun and wild activity with a young, nubile woman. Wouldn't that make a change?'

Her eyes narrowed. He meant that. 'Work?' she repeated stupidly.

'Afraid of doing anything that doesn't entail lying on your back?' he scathed.

She tightened her mouth ominously. 'I've worked harder than you can ever imagine,' she countered, stung by the taunt.

'Not in the kind of work I'm suggesting. No body contact. No stripping off for men. How does that sound?'

'Like heaven,' she said cautiously. Her mind raced. He wanted to reform her! A wry smile touched her lips, lifting the once ever-laughing corners which had recently been levelled with pain and fear.

Her impulse was to tell him to take a running jump. But suddenly there was a crack in the wall that had been blocking sight of her goal. He felt guilty. It boded well. 'What kind of work are you talking about?' she asked stiffly.

He continued to assess her for a second or two. 'Do you actually *like* decorating?'

It was difficult for Mariann not to let out a burst of astonished laughter. Her hopes soared. Tycoon feels guilt. Tycoon offers call-girl honest work. Tycoon feels better. And so would she! Lionel, she thought, I can help you.

'I love it,' she said, straight-faced.

'This has been a very difficult experience for you, it appears,' he said quietly. 'Finding me less malleable than you expected, more——'

'Lecherous, violent, brutal?' she suggested.

His eyes became glacial. 'Careful,' he said softly. 'I can still throw you into a snowdrift or heave you into the Danube and hold you under till the bubbles cease! I'm suffering from an intense frustration and that would go some way to relieving it! However, I'm not entirely ruling out the possibility that you were set up, as well as me. You took on this job without knowing the consequences. You had no idea my wife would come in, did you?'

'No,' she said shortly. 'I certainly didn't. I wouldn't have been within ten miles of you if I had.'

'I suppose you were only doing your job,' he said, sounding as though he was trying to convince himself that he was doing the right thing in not throwing her out on the street. 'I know you began that decorating to gain access to my flat and therefore me,' he continued slowly, 'but you obviously have some experience in decorating—and rather well, too.' Mariann held her breath, waiting, not daring to interrupt. He was persuading himself without her help. 'I don't want to know how you got taken on by that firm of decorators, but I imagine it's a temporary arrangement?'

'Yes,' she said demurely. Maybe she could buy time. Even if she couldn't get the keys tonight, she'd have other opportunities, the way things were working out.

'You're on the premises already, partway through the work ... It seems crazy to hire someone else when I want the place finished quickly.'

Impatiently she wished he'd stop thinking out loud and say he wanted to make amends. 'Yes,' she said encouragingly.

'What I'm suggesting,' he said at last, 'is that I let you and the men finish the offices, then move on to work on my apartment. When you've completed the job, I'll see if I can get you similar work elsewhere.'

Despite expecting this offer, Mariann was still overwhelmed at the turn in her fortunes. 'I—I'm stunned!' she breathed. It was exactly what she'd wanted ... yet contrarily she felt guilty at deceiving him. Then she crushed her conscience. She was being soft. He'd deceived a long line of women in achieving his ends and put her through degradation. 'But ... after what's happened I'd have thought you'd want me to walk away and never set eyes on me again!'

'I'm crazy,' he muttered darkly. Then, 'I don't like to see a woman selling her body.'

You *used* me! she wanted to say, contemptuous that he was like all men—riddled with double standards, denouncing immorality while indulging in it. If only she could tear strips off him, leave him bleeding and walk out! she thought vehemently—and then checked her frighteningly violent reaction.

'Could have fooled me,' she contented herself with.

'I don't use call-girls the way other men use a six-pack,' he said tightly. 'The last thing I want is a woman who jumps at my every bidding. I've no idea how you got into this sordid business and I don't want to hear. But it's a filthy world. You should get out of it. I'm offering you a chance.'

'I don't like it any more than you do,' she muttered truthfully.

'Then we're halfway there. Women should never think of themselves as material objects, to be used, bought, sold,' he said passionately.

'That's how men treat us,' she said recklessly.

'Is that all you've known?' His eyes glittered. 'It's no wonder, I suppose. You invite desire, raging passions... Knowingly or not, your body is utterly provocative, your face, your eyes...' He licked his lips and scowled. 'You're beautiful, you have an independent mind. Some might say it was decidedly stubborn. You should value yourself more. You might gain some respect for yourself—and for men—if you treated yourself better.'

'Oh!' she said feebly, astonished. 'I don't know what to say!'

'For God's sake!' he barked. 'You can stop your way of life now! You don't have to end up raddled and degraded with no self-respect, sinking eventually to selling yourself for a few Deutschmarks or forints to the tourists on the "black train". You *have* to agree with what I'm suggesting. Look into the future! Your beauty won't last——'

'Vigadó!' she cried in astonishment at his vehemence. 'You almost sound as though you're waging a personal crusade——'

His brows flew together in a fierce anger. 'Don't be crass! Just be grateful that I'm not turning you over to the *Rendörség* for false pretences!' he said in biting tones.

'The police!' she cried anxiously. 'No, don't do that! I am grateful. I'll work for you. Hard. I promise!' She'd do her best, she thought. Before she vanished.

He made an attempt to steady his rapid breathing and calm down. 'You'd better! It won't be an easy option,' he said grimly. 'But you must stick at it. If I catch you offering home comforts to Antal or any of my staff, I'll *crucify* you!' he added savagely. 'No man is to touch you! Understand?'

'Absolutely.' Mariann nodded, unnerved by the threat. But she had nothing to fear. It was one promise she could keep.

'This is only the start. You'll be tempted to earn easy money... I imagine,' he mused, 'that your usual job brings in more than a decorator could earn.'

'You're right,' she admitted drily. 'It does.'

'Think of it this way. You may be less well off, but you'll be in charge of your life and you won't feel used,' he said shortly. 'It's about time you did something honest and above board for a change.'

'Yes,' she said in a strained voice. 'That would be nice.' And she wished she could tear her gaze from his stern, mortifyingly disapproving eyes. Because she felt an absolute heel.

'Excellent,' he grunted. The glorious undulations of his bronzed satin chest loomed closer.

She tried to dismiss the uncomfortable jolt she felt in her solar plexus and leaned back. She only had to stick around for a few days before she could escape this unnervingly charismatic rat and dash back to the safety of Lionel's office.

Except that nowhere would be safe when Vigadó found out he'd been duped. Somehow, she had the feeling that he'd be prepared to follow anyone who crossed him to the ends of the earth. Heaven help her if he tried to track her down. And may God help her if he subsequently found her.

He had risen, his mission to convert her accomplished. 'Relax for a moment,' he said curtly. 'I'll take a shower and dress and make sure you get home safely.'

'There's no need——' She stopped.

He wasn't listening. His fingers had knocked against the face-down photograph and he'd stiffened. With shaking fingers, he touched the silver frame in a wistful gesture. Under his breath he murmured a term of endearment with such heartfelt sorrow that she felt an instant compassion.

Love. Sweetheart. He adored his wife, that was indisputable. Remembering how Tanya and István had stubbornly denied what was startlingly obvious to everyone, Mariann wondered if she'd ever understand the pain that lovers put each other through.

'Oh, Vigadó!' she said in exasperation. 'You fool! You love her, don't you?'

Ashen-face, he whirled to face her. 'What?'

'I heard you,' she said gently, her eyes filled with compassion. 'I believe that's a picture of your wife— and I know you called her "sweetheart". I'm at a loss to understand what's going on between you both, or what caused the spite you've been venting on one another. But you love her, that's evident. Go after her, if you know where she'll be. Tell her you love her, how much you need her. I can see you're upset,' she explained, when his brow furrowed in perplexity. 'It's never too late. What do you have to lose?' He didn't move. 'Say I leapt on you,' Mariann suggested earnestly. 'That you were tired, hung over, that I was in your bed before you knew it and you were so starved of human comfort that——'

He shook his head. 'You're a strange woman,' he said huskily.

'Hurry!' she urged plaintively. 'If you care!'

'I care. My God, how I care!' There was a silence for a moment. 'I think there's something you should know,' he said in strangled tones. He opened a drawer and swept the photo-frame into it then closed it with a decisive thud. 'After what's just happened, it will all come out into the open so I have no reason to keep silent. My "wife" is not my wife. We were divorced almost three years ago.'

'Three years?' Mariann cried in astonishment. 'But why maintain the deception that you were still married— when you hate dishonesty?'

'I had to,' he said grimly.

'I can't see anyone twisting your arm,' she said wryly.

For some time he studied her and then slowly, haltingly the words came out. 'It suited me...to keep the divorce...a secret.'

'And your ex-wife?'

A pause. A shrug of his expressive shoulders. Mariann felt he wasn't intending to tell her the whole truth.

'Eva wanted... She felt humiliated...' Vigadó scowled. 'It suited her too, for various reasons—and my father-in-law. I said I'd keep up the pretence providing I remained managing director of Dieter Ringel.'

'You got a good deal out of it,' she observed coldly.

'Did I?' he asked bleakly.

'Everyone dances to your tune,' she said.

'Always,' Vigadó agreed. 'Black and white, you said. That's what I am. No grey. Love or hate. Control or nothing.'

She shivered at his grim obsession. 'And people treated you like a married couple. That must have been strange.'

'It gave us both some protection from serious gold-diggers. We have the kind of wealth that others will lie, cheat and toady for. I spent half my time at parties peeling off female limpets.'

'Hence your contempt for women,' she said quietly.

'Oh, yes,' he said bitterly. 'You see them falling over themselves, pushing each other out of the way to reach the wealthy men in the room. You see how false they are, ready to sell their souls for riches. Money seems to affect people's sense of balance,' he muttered contemptuously. 'Even the wives of happily married friends make overtures to me whenever Eva's back's turned.'

'Have you ever thought it might be you they're interested in and not your money?' Mariann smiled wryly to herself when she said that. Whether he had money or not, he was the most magnetic male she'd ever met. Naturally women would be floored by his extraordinary charisma.

He shrugged. 'Me? No. I have no illusions. I know greed when I see it. People think money and power can cure all ills and open up a glittering, golden world.'

'But?' she prompted gently.

He seemed about to make a comment, then changed his mind. 'I'm showering. Do you want your clothes?' he asked huskily.

'Thank you.' She took the hint. He didn't want to discuss his disillusionment with the world he'd struggled so hard to inhabit. But he seemed reluctant to go, his fingers lingering on the satin gleam of the drawer that held the photograph of the woman he loved. Mariann's sad face lifted to his. There was nothing but despair in his expression. His features sagged with it, his eyes were dead. He loved his ex-wife and regretted the divorce bitterly. There *was* good in the man if he could feel such deep emotions.

'I'm so sorry about your marriage,' she said, her heart going out to him. 'I wish I could offer you hope, or comfort.'

He tightened his mouth, overcome by emotion. 'Constant hope, never fulfilled, can be worse than coming to terms with certain rejection,' he said bitterly. The broad shoulders lifted and fell with his expressive shrug. 'I've spent three years wishing, wondering, waiting. Appointments were broken. I'd fly from one side of the world to the other and find... She'd fail to turn up. She was punishing me in the only way she knew how.'

'Had you...?' She paused, delicately searching for the right words. 'Had you been unfaithful to your wife?'

He gave a faint, mirthless laugh. 'I suppose you could say I'd committed the crime of not giving Eva what she wanted—total surrender and constant attention,' he said, his tone ironic. 'Taking second place was a new experience for my wife,' he muttered. His eyes bored into Mariann's. 'What would you do if your husband didn't make love to you?' he demanded suddenly.

'Bolt the door and show him my red satin undies,' she answered wryly.

'Yes. Well you know how to arouse men, don't you?'

'It's not that,' she said. 'I mean I wouldn't give up on him without a darn good fight.'

Vigadó's lashes lowered to cover his eyes. 'This was a situation that neither of us could salvage. I couldn't stand it any longer,' he said hoarsely. 'The returned gifts, not being there for her birthday... So I decided to cut the tie once and for all.'

Now she understood. 'That's how you used me,' she said quietly. 'As a means to an end. You wanted evidence of your philandering.'

'Yes. It was a spur-of-the-moment decision. In my bed was a woman who'd willingly hired out her body. Eva was on her way up to the flat. Ironically, I believe that the person who'd hired you had mistakenly thought he could use you to smash my non-existent marriage. He thought that by doing so he could break the power of Dieter Ringel as a leading publisher,' he replied harshly.

'I think you've got it wrong,' she said. Into her mind came a treacherous thought. Lionel would have been very pleased to hurt Vigadó in that way. She tried to dismiss the idea, but it sat inside her head, niggling away. But Lionel hadn't known Vigadó would be in Budapest. She relaxed her tense muscles in relief. It would shatter her belief in human nature to discover that her boss had deceived her and set her up for Vigadó's lecherous advances.

'It ties in with a warning I'd had.' Mariann stiffened. That could have been Liz, believing Lionel might do something about Mary. 'And so I chose to twist the situation,' added Vigadó.

'By making sure we ended up in bed,' she said coldly, flushing because her vanity had led her to believe that he'd wanted her. Instead, he'd manipulated her completely, his arousal being a natural by-product of her writhing!

'It happened,' he drawled, 'because I allowed it.'

'Does nothing happen in your life unless you permit it?' she muttered.

'Nothing.' He hesitated. Then he spoke more softly, a heavy timbre in his throbbing voice. 'Almost nothing.'

'You could win your ex-wife back,' she said shakily. This man could win any woman he wanted. Even the betrayed Eva.

'No. I would never try. I'll have to excise...' He caught his breath, cleared his throat and tried unsuccessfully to steady his voice. 'I must wipe her from my life, my memories.'

Inexplicably, she wanted to cry for him. He was being as ruthless with himself as he was with others. But it was hurting. That was obvious. Hesitating for only a brief moment, she wrapped the covers around her and went to him, startling him by simply holding his shoulders tightly, a sympathetic, human gesture that she hoped would alleviate some of the loneliness he must be feeling.

'When she knows how much you're grieving——' she began gently.

'No. Never!' he cried hoarsely. 'I wouldn't give her the satisfaction. It's finished.'

'You must keep your memories,' she said softly. 'Never lose sight of the good times.'

'Reminders would be too painful.' He looked down at her, a puzzled expression on his face. 'I can't believe you're doing this,' he muttered. 'Or that I'm standing here, letting you comfort me.'

'Why not? You need it,' she replied with warm logic.

'I suppose your clients talk to you a lot,' he said with a frown. 'You know their sexual preferences so they feel safe to tell you their secrets.'

Discomfited, she touched her lips with the tip of her tongue. It wasn't easy being cast in the role of a re-formed call-girl, she thought ruefully. 'People do talk to me,' she agreed quietly. 'They think I have an experience of the world they don't share. When they're down, they look to me to cheer them up. Speaking of which, you mustn't give up hope——'

'I knew what I was doing,' he rasped. 'I know her. I broke our arrangement. I can't expect mercy. She's ruthless, like her father. Like me. She'll never forgive me.'

'But I can't believe you'd deliberately deny yourself the woman you love!' she cried, bewildered by the remorselessness of his denial of all hope.

Vigadó inhaled deeply and looked deep into her eyes. 'I've lived in a prison for the whole of my married life,' he said quietly. 'It began badly, continued badly, ended badly. But I've had a debt to pay to Dieter. He trained me, taught me the business. So I stayed and learnt lessons no one else could offer. More and more I've come to rant and rail against that prison. I've wanted to be free. I've wanted to stop appearing in public with Eva, smiling, chatting to her and going through the lie that we were married. The deceit has made me feel less than human. It took away my dignity, my pride.'

Mariann refrained from reminding him of his less than honest commercial coups. This wasn't the time. 'You'd choose freedom and personal integrity over love?' she asked quietly.

His eyes dropped. 'Every time,' he growled. 'Every damn time. Only gibbering fools inflict pain on themselves and let themselves be manipulated by the fickle game of love.'

Those had been her sentiments too. Yet faced with the reality of his empty future—and what that must mean to him—she wasn't sure she believed that any more. 'But you hurt,' she said hesitantly. 'You say you don't want the pain that love brings, but you're feeling pain now.' His eyes were quite guarded. A lie, she thought intuitively. He's going to tell me a lie.

'I'll get over it,' he said hoarsely.

And she knew he never would. An overwhelming urge swept through her to be the one who made him forget, who taught him that life could be fun again and that hearts could mend. Rocked by her impulse, she subdued it hastily. Vigadó was like the rest of her family. Consumed with passion. Either he loved Eva, or he wouldn't love anyone. Ever.

He gave her a bleak smile and Mariann's heart turned over. For a long time they stared at one another, the atmosphere seeming to thicken and soften with languid warmth around them. She held her breath when his lips parted because she sensed he was about to say something momentous.

To her eternal regret, he snapped his mouth shut and smiled, touching her hair instead, but with such wistfulness that she found herself smiling gently back.

'What a woman!' he mused. 'Sharp and sassy, with God knows what experience of life and the seamier side of sex, but, despite all that, underneath...' his accent began to take on the quality of a caress '...somehow you've kept sight of compassion.'

Crazily, she wanted to kiss him. Instead, she forced a grin. 'Tart with a heart of gold,' she quipped. 'Don't you ever watch old movies? And you are a puppy dog with a loud bark.'

He managed a weak grin. 'Am I? Perhaps,' he conceded. 'Most of the time I'm waiting to bite.'

'They say a dog will bite if he senses fear,' she smiled.

'And respect strength and courage,' he said softly. 'Only a woman like you, someone who's tough and has come up the hard way, would recognise that there's more to me than a bark and sharp teeth.' His head angled to one side. 'I imagine we've had the same kind of background—hard, unyielding.' Gently, his arms slid around her. 'That produces survivors. No wonder I feel a strange link with you. We're very alike.'

'We're not!' she cried indignantly.

'You're a fighter,' he said softly. 'You ruthlessly cover up your wounds and lick them in private. And, despite the profession you chose, you hate being dominated. You have more courage than most men I know. And more sex-appeal in the sweep of your eyelashes on those pale gold cheekbones than most women have in their whole bodies. We're two of a kind, you and I. That binds us together.'

No, she thought in dismay. It can't do that! He was her sworn enemy and she had yet to cheat him, to rifle through his office files, to ease his favourite new author away from his clutches and...and to deceive him. The very idea filled her with an appalled reluctance.

She groaned. She'd become involved. The last thing she should have done. 'My clothes,' she reminded him shakily. 'I need to clear up. And eat. I'm famished.'

'I could order something,' he suggested quietly. 'Outlaw soup, carp, steak...?'

The prospect of food for one of her hungers was wonderful. But she dared not stay. The relationship between them had become fraught with pitfalls. And she didn't trust herself.

'No, thanks. I'll munch my sandwiches on the way home and get something there,' she said casually.

'As you like. I'll fetch your clothes. Give me five minutes to shower. Then I'll escort you home.'

'Oh, no...' She let her voice trail away and tried not to look where the keys must be. He'd ruin her plans!

'I insist.'

There was no denying him, that was obvious. With a heavy sigh, she resigned herself to searching another time. 'But...' How could she let him take her to the Hilton? István had insisted that she borrow his permanent suite, saying it would be excellent for business meetings. She hadn't enlightened him. Both he and Tanya had jumped to the conclusion that she was in Budapest to initiate links with Eastern Europe and bring some more business in for Lionel's ailing publishing company.

'Ashamed of your home?' he asked, his eyes narrowed.

'Don't be daft. Take me to Disz tér,' she said as evenly as she could. 'I can get a taxi from there.'

'Done,' he agreed lazily. 'But from the moment you begin work tomorrow, you'll be under my wing, as my protégée. You'll have my protection. And I mean to keep you on the straight and narrow by ensuring that I know where you are twenty-four hours a day.'

Mariann's hazel eyes widened in alarm. It was a condition she couldn't allow. She needed the freedom to come and go if she was to do a proper hunt for Mary's address. With Vigadó spying on her with those all-seeing eyes of his, she'd have no chance of gathering the information she needed.

Vigadó threw her clothes on the bed. She waited till she heard the shower being turned on and the sounds of splashing. With her heart in her mouth, she stole over and foraged through his trouser pockets. No keys. Nor were they anywhere in the room as far as she could discover. Feeling defeated, she dressed. Every time she made an effort, she was thwarted. And life was getting more hairy every day.

A small, persistent voice told her there was another reason for the trembling of her body. Vigadó was dangerous. Not only because he had an unnerving quality of seeing through deceit, but because he sent her common sense spinning into orbit. A look, a touch, and she melted. Her own personal integrity was at stake if she spent time in his company.

Some time soon she'd have to decide whether to risk his seduction, or abandon her task and flee with her virginity intact. And suddenly, however crazy the idea was, she felt a terrible certainty that, in denying herself Vigadó's love-making, she'd be denying everything she'd ever desired in a man.

All or nothing. That would be the choice. Yes; how mortifyingly alike they were!

CHAPTER SIX

OUTSIDE it was icy cold after the warmth of the apartment, and Mariann paused in the cobbled courtyard to raise the hood of her shocking-pink ski-jacket and to snuggle the white fur trimming against her face.

Across the other side of the medieval yard, taunting her with its nearness, were the studded doors that led to the offices. Window grilles in fine wrought iron, heavy wooden shutters and the presence of a burglar alarm rendered the whole building Mariann-proof. No chance of a night foray.

'It's like Alcatraz over there! What do you keep in those offices, gold-bound copies of first editions?' she joked. 'One man could conduct a siege single-handed from the building,' she added drily.

'He probably did,' smiled Vigadó. 'The whole hill was under siege three hundred years ago. Most of the buildings were in ruins by the end of it. See those stone lions and the Gothic arches? They're the medieval remains, incorporated into the eighteenth-century stonework. And when they rebuilt the town,' he said, patting a massive stone quoin, 'it was with a fear of the Turks and a siege mentality, which resulted in buildings which are beautiful but tough—a little like you,' he said softly.

'You don't have to worry about burglars, then,' she said, quite flattered by his remark.

'Just as well,' he drawled. 'My competitors would be queuing up to ransack my databases otherwise.'

'Databases?' she queried sharply. Lionel had talked about files. Files were things you lifted out of filing cabinets. She could cope with them. Databases were on computers—and accessible only via passwords!

'We're not totally computerised and data-linked into London and New York at this end,' he conceded. 'But will be, in a short time. Give me your arm,' he said to the dismayed Mariann. 'There'll be a layer of ice beneath this fresh snow from where the janitor cleared the yard earlier. It'll be treacherous and I don't want you to fall.'

'Thanks, but I'm perfectly fit,' she said absently. She made mental plans to work overtime every night so that she could have a free run of the offices as soon as possible. Even if she couldn't get hold of their mailing list, there must be letters from Mary filed somewhere—or a recent one, lying on a desk unfiled, since she was close to finishing her novel. She was a great letter-writer. Mariann's spirits rose sky-high with hope.

'As I said, you're tough,' he murmured.

'Not enough men realise that,' she said darkly. 'I'm keen to get your offices finished. Do you mind if I'm in at eight tomorrow?'

'No problem. I'll leave instructions for you to be let in. Arrive whenever you want. I'll have been working for an hour by that time,' he said.

She hid her annoyance. 'That'll give your staff a shock!' she exclaimed.

'It's intended to,' he answered drily. 'How else do I get the best out of everyone?'

'Affection?' she suggested.

He grunted derisively. 'That's something I don't know much about. Nor do I want to.'

'Why?' she asked bluntly.

'It fogs the brain.'

'You're only saying that because...' Her voice gentled. 'Because you're hurting so much, you want to deny what you feel for your wife.'

'Don't interpret my behaviour from your point of view,' he said coldly. 'You'll miss the truth by a long way. Affection is a burden. It distracts you from your purpose and makes you vulnerable to the machinations of others. If I ever showed weakness,' he growled, 'I know there would be enough unscrupulous bastards around to slip daggers into any exposed parts of my flesh and twist the blades till I bled to death.'

If that was the price of success, she thought soberly, she didn't want to be a billionaire! But it grieved her that Vigadó should reject human affection because he saw it as a weakness to be conquered. How like István he was! she mused. Two men, both quite merciless with themselves, driving themselves towards a non-existent 'perfection'.

Yet Tanya had reached out and touched István with her love. Mariann's face softened with tenderness and she realised to her surprise that she was wishing fervently that Vigadó could experience a love as sweet and as life-changing as Tanya's.

'So you rule like a merciless Turkish pasha, through fear,' she said quietly.

His mouth twisted. 'But I *rule*,' he said tersely. She trembled at his hunger for power and hoped he never decided to control her. 'Glad you're on my side?' he murmured.

Mariann gave a rueful laugh. 'I don't think anyone's on your side. I think you stand for yourself and no one else.'

'I think you're right,' he said softly. 'That makes me very dangerous, doesn't it?' He studied her face for a moment or two while she tried to mask her sense of apprehension. 'You're shivering,' he husked. 'Come.'

His arm came around her shoulder and drew her to the warmth of his body. She had a contrary feeling of wanting to stay, wrapped in his sheltering, illogically protective embrace, and yet wanting to break away and show her independence.

She stayed. Showing, she told herself, that he posed no dangers for her since she was immune.

They walked beneath the low, deep arch which had once admitted horse-drawn coaches into the cobbled courtyard. As if by mutual agreement, they stopped to listen to the peace of the silent world that sat high above the city and to breathe in the clean, champagne air. Both she and Vigadó stared up at the diamond-sharp stars, so searingly bright in the hard black sky that their beauty made her catch her breath.

'It's enchanting. What a wonderful place to work and live!' She sighed.

'Certainly to work,' he mused. 'As for living...' His voice trailed away, uncharacteristically.

A spasm must have lanced through his body and tightened every one of his muscles. Mariann realised he was still concealing his distress about Eva. Her gloved hand squeezed his arm. 'You'll find love again and start living, one day,' she said gently, wishing this hard man would ease up on himself. 'You said you were a survivor. You must risk showing Eva your vulnerability and tell her how much you love her. She'll be overwhelmed, I promise. You can achieve anything you want.'

He took her hand in his with a faint smile, his fingers absently smoothing the scarlet leather. 'I can,' he said quietly. 'I will. And so will you.'

Mariann gave a nervous laugh and tugged at his arm to go. If she achieved her aim, she thought ruefully, it would shock Vigadó into a violent reaction. Her stomach churned at the prospect.

Silent with their own thoughts, they crunched across the fresh snow. It crackled beneath Mariann's red ankle boots and for a while that was the only sound in the muffled night. They left the sheltered street and turned into the square by the huge Matthias church.

'That wind's from Siberia,' she gasped.

Vigadó cuddled her more closely and hurried her to the lee of the statue of St Stephen on horseback, the whole of which was shrouded from the frost by an enormous, ghostly sheet. 'Here,' he said, slipping off his scarf and tying it around the outside of her collar for extra warmth. 'Your legs must be freezing. Will these things pull up?'

Before she could demur, he'd bent and begun to ease up her tangerine leg-warmers till they covered her shocking-pink ski-pants from ankle to thigh. And while he did so Mariann gazed down on his beautiful glossy head and felt an overwhelming urge to cradle it in her hands, to lift his face, crouch down in front of him and gently kiss those smoky lids with their enviable thick lashes that were fluttering so heart-wrenchingly sweetly on his cheeks.

Instead, she pretended to be examining the stars and stolidly forced herself to endure the touch of his gloved fingers on her spread thighs.

'Orange and shriek-pink,' he murmured, rising perilously close to her. 'Bright, innit?' he teased.

Mariann laughed in surprised delight. 'Love my colour combination or loathe it——'

'I love it,' he said huskily. 'You're so *obvious*. No problem seeing you against the pure white snow, is there?'

Was that a dig at her 'morals'? On a sudden impulse, still fired with unshed energy that needed dissipating, she bent and formed a snowball, hurling it directly into his face before he realised what she was doing. Then she began to run, knowing she'd done something foolish. You didn't throw snowballs at billionaire bosses!

'Ouch!' she cried as a huge snowy missile thudded into the back of her head. Billionaires evidently retaliated! Whirling around in glee, she scooped up two handfuls of snow and was caught by another direct hit, full in the face, as she crouched down. 'Beast!' she yelled, gasping and clearing her vision.

The laughing Vigadó dodged behind a lamp-post. 'I fight to win!' he called, ducking hastily.

'So do I!' she retorted, surprising him with a left-hander.

'I'm more ruthless than you!' He ran towards her, unheeding of the barrage of snow she wildly hurled at him before she took fright and turned tail, darting to the cloisters of the Fishermen's bastion where she ran headlong, weak with laughter, till she found herself trapped against a wall.

She turned, her hands flat against the cold stone, and saw that he'd disappeared.

Cautiously, she gathered a heap of snow together and packed it hard. There was a silence. She listened, her head on one side. Nothing, only the wind, beginning to shriek around the turrets of the bastion. Then she saw footprints and began to follow them and suddenly a dark figure was creeping up the steps that led to one of the fairy-tale towers. With a laugh to dispel her slight apprehension, she padded silently after it, hugging the walls so that she stayed in the shadows.

She stopped at the top to listen again. Nothing. It seemed that she was completely alone, the whole Castle Hill deserted. 'Vigadó?' she ventured a little nervously. 'Where are you?'

'Above you,' came the whisper.

She looked up, was swamped in a miniature avalanche of snow and was left gasping and laughing from the cold douche till a pair of warm hands wielding a large handkerchief helped sweep the icy crystals from her face.

'You don't play fair!' she spluttered.

'No,' he agreed softly. 'I never do. Because I always have to win.'

And he kissed her.

For a moment she clung to his warmth and then pushed away, her eyes dark with confusion at the laughter in his eyes. 'Fie, Mr Billionaire!' she managed to chide. 'What would your business colleagues think of you, having snowball fights and pursuing a gaudy woman in shriek-pink?'

'They'd see how I apply myself with equal dedication to anything I do. And, recognising my tenacity, they'd quite rightly shake in their shoes,' he murmured.

It was a warning, she thought. Intentional or not. 'Don't take up the escort business or decorating,' she said tartly, trying to stay in character. 'I couldn't stand the competition.'

He grinned. 'Acknowledging my superiority, are you?'

'Oh, no,' she answered with haughty confidence. '*My* work is enhanced by the application of my warm heart and loving soul. Qualities you lack.'

'And because of that fact they're qualities I could destroy if I wished.'

Mariann froze at the sinister threat and stubbornly made herself smile perkily so that he didn't see she was rattled. There was something barbaric in this man that made him want to flatten anything and anyone that stood up to him.

'You can't reach them,' she said defiantly.

'Don't tempt me to prove you wrong.'

Her breathing quickened. Time to bow out. She laughed gaily and brushed snow from his lapel—a controlling gesture, a motherly one that had helped her to crush cocksure Don Juans in the past.

This one grabbed her hand. Ripped off the scarlet glove. Turned her hand over. Kissed the palm, slowly, intimately, disregarding her attempts to pull away, his tongue tracing in warm spirals the soft lines and the thick pad beneath the thumb, gently savaging the flesh now with his sharp teeth. Heat in her body flowed from spinning head to wriggling toes, intense enough, she thought wildly, to have melted her into a pool of steaming liquid.

His eyebrow lifted in challenge as he released her hand, daring her to deny his infernal skill.

'You're an accomplished lover, I'm sure,' she said, willing her voice to remain steady. 'But sex and lust have nothing to do with hearts and souls and that's why you can rule people but not win their hearts. And why you're missing out on so much in life, because you refuse to acknowledge the fundamental thing that makes life worthwhile——'

'Love?' he scorned.

'You know it exists!' she protested. 'You can't deny that——'

'But I do. You think you know what I feel for Eva. You're wrong,' he said harshly. 'It isn't love. It never was. It was something more fundamentally primitive than that.'

'If it was lust, you wouldn't be hurt now——'

'You don't know the whole story,' he muttered impatiently. 'It's more complicated than you imagine. I had certain . . . needs. Eva was willing to fulfil them.'

Mariann blanched, her imagination running riot. Vigadó's passions must be pretty wild. 'Oh,' she said weakly.

'Take it from me, love doesn't exist, not between man and woman,' said Vigadó bitterly. 'It's a delusion created to encourage the species to mate and reproduce itself. After a few years of enforced living together, the scales fall from people's eyes and love vanishes.'

She smiled, sadly. 'Sometimes,' she conceded. 'But not if the right choice has been made. Love does exist,' she said huskily. 'It was there between my parents for the whole of their lives, it's been there for years between my brother and the girl next door. And also between my sister and... and the man she's engaged to,' she said, carefully not mentioning István's name. 'It will exist for me too because I want to love someone——'

'You'll persuade yourself, delude yourself,' he muttered.

'No!' she said hotly. 'I'll know how to recognise it. But I don't think it will play a part in your life if you keep denying it.'

'Quite a philosopher call-girl, aren't you?' he snapped.

And, angry though she was, she knew she'd hit home, wounded him. He hated to think that other people were enjoying the ultimate pleasure that he might never experience. 'I'll walk the rest of the way on my own,' she said with quiet dignity.

'You could stay. Spend the night with me and teach me about love.'

His tone and his face were so deadpan that she didn't know if he was joking or serious. She opted for joking. 'Or I could go home and fry potatoes,' she said airily, pretending to consider the two options. 'Don't be offended, but I think I'd prefer chips.'

Vigadó laughed but she sensed he'd logged her rejection in his little black book of pending punishments. 'You don't know what you're missing,' he murmured.

'I can hazard a guess,' she said wryly. 'You're into bondage. You'd have me bound hand and foot to your bed before I could get my boots off!'

'Damn! My dastardly plan uncovered!' he said, smiting his forehead in mock-despair.

'Foiled again, oh, white slaver! Goodnight, Vigadó, I must dash!' She grinned, surprised at how he'd refused to show annoyance at the way she'd evaded him. That was pride, she thought. He'd never admit to defeat. 'I'm going weak at the knees thinking of those chips.'

With a cheery wave, she strode in the direction of the taxi rank. He followed; she could hear the crunch of fresh snow beneath his feet. So she turned, placing her hand on her hips aggressively.

'Carry on,' he said calmly. 'I'll be right behind you every step of the way. I'm enough of a gentleman to make sure you reach the safety of your taxi.'

Mariann shrugged, hoping he didn't extend his concern much further than that and follow her to her destination. Somehow she had to get back to her hotel that night without Vigadó knowing.

At the rank, he chatted in a friendly way to the driver in Hungarian while Mariann slipped into the warm car. To her relief, Vigadó waved casually and strode away without a backward glance. She asked the driver to wait a moment. When Vigadó was out of sight she apologised, said she'd changed her mind and slipped the man a good tip before jumping out and hurrying through the back streets to the Hilton, unseen by anyone.

Or so she fervently hoped.

Several days later, after getting over his disappointment that her hair wasn't naturally blonde and Marilynish, Antal sidled up to Mariann while she and her fellow decorators were shifting the furniture from the editors' offices.

'You need a break, all that hard work. Shall we have a coffee?' he suggested huskily.

A stream of bristling Hungarian cracked out from behind them both and they turned to see Vigadó snapping out instructions in all directions. Antal began to make some excuses, but Vigadó spat a few words at him, barked a few more orders and everyone leapt about energetically, like ponies around a circus trainer.

'A word,' he said to Mariann, jerked his head at her and strode off down the corridor towards his office.

'Follow!' said Antal urgently, when she failed to make a move.

'In my own good time,' she muttered stubbornly. Hauling out a bar of chocolate from her bag, she slowly unpeeled the wrapper and foil. She took a satisfyingly large bite and began to wander down the corridor, munching on the rich, dark chocolate and wondering what side of bed Vigadó had got out of that morning.

He'd foiled all her attempts to make a search for stray letters, let alone the more elusive, safeguarded keys. He'd begun work early and never left till well after ten at night, after making sure that she'd left the premises. No wonder he was bad-tempered and sour, she mused, if he worked without a break.

Once, he'd asked the friendly, easygoing András—the senior of the two men with her—to estimate the decorating cost for his apartment, and suggested she go to make some suggestions for colour schemes. By pretending to be making notes, when she'd already decided in an instant what scheme she'd recommend, she'd had time for another search. Fruitless.

Annoyed, she'd called her father then her sister Sue for a quick chat and, consumed with curiosity, had tried the number Lionel had given her. She'd found herself connected to a woman who was, apparently, running a call-girl business.

That had left her with two possibilities. Either Lionel had made a mistake in giving her the number, or it had been intentional. But if Lionel had set her up—and the idea was unthinkable; how could she have considered it?—she failed to see what purpose that would serve.

'*Reggelt*!' She smiled, bidding good morning to a crowd of men fitting new desk units. Changes were happening fast. Vigadó's work schedule had been an eye-opener after Lionel's leisurely pace. Thinking of which, she mused, she *must* ring Lionel's secretary today and get the right contact number, since she'd been unable to reach him.

'Oh, there you are,' she mumbled, still chomping on chocolate as she surveyed the dark, brooding figure in the beautifully furnished office. It looked more like a study, it was so comfortable. The legend on the door no longer said 'Antal Millassin'. It appeared Vigadó had definitely taken up residence in his manager's old office.

'In.'

With a silent sigh of resignation, Mariann stepped into the spacious room and closed the heavy door. Vigadó was leaning back in a plush leather chair, his feet on an enormous antique desk, its surface awash with papers and magazines. Her eyes gleamed. There was a stock of manuscripts to one side. She walked forward and sat in the chair nearest to them, very prim, her legs neatly together, her hands folded in her lap. He wanted submissive, she'd act it. But not *be* it.

'Did you like my suggestions for upstairs?' she asked in a conversational tone, trying to angle her head so that she could flick surreptitious glances at the manuscripts.

'Excellent,' he said grudgingly. 'I've taken up your suggestion that the bedroom would look less like a brothel if the fabrics were more subtle. Someone's making up sheets and drapes in blues and silver-greys.'

'I thought it needed toning down,' she said wryly.

'You're not wearing anything under that boiler suit.'

She blinked at his rapid change of tack. 'How do you know?'

'The way your body moves.' He scowled. 'Others will notice, too——'

'I'm *hot*!' she complained.

'So is Antal, if I interpret the look in his eye,' he said cynically. 'Though I'll keep him busy today and out of your hair. And tomorrow you'll make your body less...mobile. It might not be your style to wear underwear, but you're not supposed to be provocative any more.' The tip of his tongue touched his sultry upper lip. 'Or instantly available,' he added huskily. 'Understand?'

'Yes.' She sighed, absently taking an unladylike bite of chocolate and manoeuvring it awkwardly around her

mouth. 'Are these from your authors?' Quickly, before
he could reply, she heaved the pile to one side, splaying
them on his desk and scanning the titles. Nothing
English. They all bristled with thickly clustering con-
sonants and excited accents, Hungarian style.

'Put them back in order,' he said sharply. 'Don't touch
anything in here. While you're in the offices, I expect
you to be circumspect in the way you dress, behave, and
speak. I told you before, you are here as a decorator,
nothing else. Besides, I'm the only one around who could
afford your call-girl prices, so don't waste your time even
considering making a little money on the side.' His
phones were ringing but he ignored them, hooking his
feet off the desk and leaning forward. 'And that's why
I called you in. I have another job for you,' he said. 'In
a couple of weeks.'

'Can't make it. I won't have finished——'

'You'll do it,' he snapped curtly. 'I've got an author
coming over from Heathrow. She's a new acqui-
sition——'

'Heathrow . . . she?' queried Mariann, suddenly alert.

'She,' he said, his eyes watchful. 'Judging by the brief
meeting I had with her, she's dynamite. I'm going to
show her around, get to know her and establish the be-
ginnings of a professional relationship.'

Could be Mary. Could be anyone. But . . . 'What will
I be doing?' she asked hopefully.

The black eyes glittered with contempt. 'You're an
expert in acting a part, in being the ideal escort. Try
your skill with your own sex for a change. You'll make
her feel at home, being British too. I want you to help
entertain her. Amuse her, take her shopping, have tea in
Gundels so I can get on with some work occasionally. I
can't spare the time to be nursemaid for a whole
weekend.'

Somehow, Mariann kept a straight face while her mind
was leaping in all directions. If this was Mary, he was
handing her his star author on a plate! She curbed her
impulse to castigate him for dishing out what he considered to be a feminine role.

'I like shopping,' she said blandly.

'Of course you do,' he said patronisingly.

'What's her name?' she asked casually. 'Will I know her?'

'Details later. Off you go.' He'd finished with her, answering both telephones simultaneously and buzzing for his secretary who came in and started to reel off information at a frightening pace.

For a few seconds, the awed Mariann watched him deal with three people at once and then she left to start laying out her dustsheets. But all the while she was wondering if fortune had favoured her at last, and she would be left in charge of Mary O'Brien for long enough to expose Vigadó for the bully he was and to coax her back to Lionel. She could afford to wait. It could be easier than picking locks.

Gradually, as the days progressed, she became aware of a quickening of pace around her and marvelled at the changes Vigadó was making. The Hungarian staff—with the exception of Antal, perhaps—already worked hard and extraordinarily long hours like all Hungarians, but they seemed determined to show their punitive boss that they could keep up an even more punishing pace than before.

His voice sounded through the offices, at first sharp and snappy then increasingly quiet and authoritative. Everyone began to work with intense dedication whether he was there or not. The translators typed more rapidly, manuscript piles sank lower, people dealt faster with phone calls, the very air buzzed with feverish activity.

Out of the corner of her eye she'd catch glimpses of Vigadó flashing by her open door, shirt-sleeves rolled up high on his brawny arms, a purposeful expression on his face. And suddenly she noticed that no one walked past any more; they half ran.

On the first day he'd sacked two secretaries on the spot for spending an hour gossiping in the cloakroom. On the second he'd firmly ejected an elegant young woman who'd pretended to be collecting for charity but was a rejected admirer of his and had tried to entice him by undoing her blouse.

On the third day he'd had a stand-up row with his father-in-law which had made the secretaries and copy-editors cover their ears in deep embarrassment—but proudly tell Mariann later over coffee that Vigadó had won concessions in management of the company and was a match for any man, even the ruthless Dieter Ringel himself.

She found it odd. Vigadó was acting like a bear and getting accolades. And loyalty. Everyone had rooted for him during the row with Dieter. Mariann had the impression that they would have collectively thrown Dieter out if Vigadó had asked. People began to hum while they worked. Then sing. And every morning she felt keen to start work and reluctant to leave, after exhilarating days of working in a highly charged, enthusiastic atmosphere, of listening to and joining in with the wonderful Hungarian folk songs that staff broke into spontaneously whenever they moved around between offices.

It had been impossible for her to get the information she needed, but she told herself it didn't matter, not when she might have Mary to herself, without any risk involved. And if not, well, she'd have to apply herself a little more.

Thoughtfully she rubbed a cherub's bottom with glasspaper, working on her own while András and János finished the fine detail work in the editors' room. Tomorrow she'd possibly be meeting Mary and talking to her. Then, successful or not, she'd be leaving, one way or the other. And why she felt sad she couldn't fathom.

'My God!' The door closed softly and when she turned her head and peered down she saw Antal, mopping his brow. 'I knew Vigadó was difficult, but he's done nothing but criticise all morning! Have lunch with me, Mimi; I need a warm heart to make me feel better.'

'I'm not taking lunch, thanks,' she said briskly, climbing down and heaving the ladder to one side. All the cherubs but one had smooth bottoms, she thought in satisfaction. They looked cute!

'Let me help with the ladder.'

Antal was beside her. And holding her hand. 'You won't move the ladder that way,' she said calmly, tugging to no avail. 'And Vigadó's told me not to bother you because you're too busy.'

'He's occupied. Talking on the phone to his new saga writer,' husked Antal.

'Oh! Who is she? Anyone I know?' asked Mariann ingenuously.

'You are interested.' Antal's hand stroked her face and she gritted her teeth against the impulse to bite his fingers. 'Everyone is fascinated by writers.'

'Mmm. I'm riveted,' she agreed, reaching out and managing to get hold of a wet paintbrush—just in case she needed him to back off. 'Tell me her name, do!'

'I will tell you for a kiss.'

It was only a mouth, she argued. Sloppy-looking, though; one she'd rather stayed ten feet away from hers, but she *did* need to know—and she did have the paint-brush handy. But...no. The thought turned her stomach.

'Don't be silly,' she said crushingly. 'I—mmmph!'

Her body slammed against Antal's, his arms wrapped around her tightly. She felt his hot breath on her face and then wet, slippery lips claiming her mouth. Recovering from the shock, she flexed her knee and drove it upwards, hard. As Antal shrieked and folded over and she grimly painted his face with dove-grey emulsion, her glittering eyes shot up to meet a pair that seemed to have been fashioned from black steel.

Vigadó's hand snaked out, turned Antal and thrust him against the wall. '*Viszontlátásra*!' he growled softly. Goodbye. And even more softly, '*Menj a tenébe*!' Go to hell!

The matt-grey Antal was bundled out before she realised he was on his way. There was a thud, the sound of a body tumbling and a cry of pain. She held her breath, wondering what had happened. When Vigadó came in again, she could see that his whole body simmered with a consuming anger.

'What did you do?' she gasped.

'Threw him down the back stairs!' he snarled.

'But...it—it was just a kiss,' she said nervously. 'And I dealt with it——'

'But other women might not,' he said tersely. 'I won't have men like that working for me.'

Her eyes widened. 'You've sacked him?'

'I made it quite clear in our first staff meeting what my reaction would be to that kind of harassment!' he snapped.

'I suppose you've never chatted up a female in the office?' she retorted scornfully.

'Never.'

'I don't believe you!' she cried. 'Antal was only trying it on! I didn't need your help! I made it quite clear that I wasn't interested——'

Vigadó came forward and roughly caught her shoulders, scowling into her eyes. 'Why are you defending him!' he seethed. 'Did you lead him on? Do you feel guilty?'

'No!' she fumed. 'But it wasn't such a crime——'

'In my books,' growled Vigadó, 'it is.'

She met his lashing gaze head-on. '*You* don't believe in the misuse of power?' she asked in scornful disbelief.

'I'm perfectly prepared to use power to get what I think is right. But I don't like people having sex in office hours when I'm paying for their time,' he said tightly. 'If it's any consolation to you, I was going to sack him anyway. He's inefficient.'

'Haven't you sacked enough people?' she said disapprovingly.

'I have now. Don't you think the office is working well? Don't your female vibes pick up a certain...eagerness and excitement in the air?' he mocked.

'Ye-e-es,' she admitted. 'Lord knows why!'

'I'll tell you, then,' he said drily. 'People like a firm hand——'

'Oh, yes,' she said sweetly. 'Women and horses.'

'They like someone who radiates confidence,' he said tightly. 'It makes them secure. This place lacked direction and leadership. I cracked the whip and brought everyone into line. They all know where they are now, what the ground rules are and how far they can go. Efficiency is high, no time is wasted and the staff are happier, prouder of what they're achieving. They loathed me at first. That was good.'

'It was?' she asked, puzzled. Vigadó's tactics were beyond her.

'Of course. It gave them someone to gang up against. They became a team for the first time and supported each other. When I eased off and they discovered I was leaving them alone as far as their individual work was concerned—*if* I was happy with what they were doing— they began to respect me. I don't ask for love,' he said sardonically. 'Respect will do. And no one would respect me if I kept Antal on. He was the cause of the decline in standards. I'm promoting Judit. She's very keen.'

Privately Mariann thought he'd made the right decision, but had no intention of saying so. 'It's your business. Excuse me,' she said politely, unsuccessfully trying to prise his fingers from her arms. 'I have to rub a cherub's bottom.'

Vigadó's mouth twitched at one corner. 'Poor Antal,' he mused, tipping up her chin with a firm forefinger. 'What chance did he stand? I'll push a month's salary his way if that makes you feel better. I can hardly blame him for risking my wrath and trying to make a pass at you. You're a tempting little piece,' he said patronisingly. 'Get your coat on.'

Mariann made her mind catch up with his abrupt change of direction again. 'Why?'

'I'm not taking you out dressed in a boiler suit covered in paint.'

'You're not taking me out, period,' she said briskly.

'We're having lunch.'

'I've eaten it.' She waved a casual arm towards two empty bags of crisps and a small bar of fruit and nut.

'How you have such a flawless complexion I don't know,' he drawled. 'I want to talk about this weekend. Why not do that while eating beef with herbs, paprika and dumplings washed down with a glass of Bikavér, sweet strudel filled with apple, nuts and cherries, Turkish coffee and plum brandy?' He folded his arms and assessed the level of her enthusiasm.

She groaned. 'Beast!' she muttered. 'You've got me drooling.'

Laughing, he removed the brush from her non-too-reluctant hand. 'If you prefer, we could have a working dinner this evening: soft candlelight, gentle music, seductive dancing——'

'No fear!' she grinned. 'You're only safe in daylight hours.' He seemed to be trying not to smile, as if even that was questionable. 'Where are we eating?' she asked, capitulating.

They sat on a terrace outside a thirteenth-century inn, much to the surprise of the proprietor, since the snow had to be brushed from the paving stones first. Vigadó had ordered a table and chairs to be carried outside and, since his reputation had already spread around the Castle district, no one even considered refusing his startling request. It was sheltered and quite lovely to bask in the winter sunshine and Mariann warmed up with a bowl of Hunter's soup before tackling the wild boar with its throat-blasting strips of red pepper.

'Gorgeous!' she sighed, pushing her plate away—and glad that Vigadó didn't waste good eating time by talking non-stop. 'Now, what about the weekend?'

'Pudding?' he suggested.

'I'd die!' she groaned. 'Apricot pancakes would be nice.'

He laughed at her weakness, lifted a hand and as if by magic a waiter appeared at his side to take the order. 'There's something I want you to do for me first,' he said lazily, leaning back in his chair and viewing her through a fringe of black lashes.

'I knew there'd be a catch,' she sighed. 'What is it?'

'Go out to Váci utca,' he said, naming the smartest shopping street in Budapest, 'and buy something simple, black and understated—with my money. Then come with me this evening to a champagne celebration. All the food you can eat, a doggie bag if you want, a seething inferno of disco dancers and a bouquet of flowers to take home afterwards.'

Mariann sipped her wine warily. 'What do I have to do for that?' she asked cynically. 'Mother told me there's no such thing as a free lunch. As for free dinner with champagne...the mind boggles!'

'I want you to stick by me.'

Her eyes widened. 'How close?' she asked suspiciously.

He waited while their pancakes were flamed and chuckled as her jaw dropped when the waiter solemnly ladled something suspiciously like pink blancmange over her helping. 'Not to your taste?' he murmured.

'I'll eat anything,' she grinned, tucking in.

'So I noticed. Not very choosy, are you?' he said smoothly.

'I'm sitting with you, aren't I?' she laughed.

'How reckless you are,' he murmured unnervingly. 'Now let me tell you about tonight. It's a meeting of financiers. Yes,' he said, seeing her nose wrinkle. 'Boring. But necessary. I want to talk business. The men's wives will want to dance. One of them in particular will be trying to fan the flames of what she fondly imagines was a thwarted affair between us. Since I no longer have a "wife" to partner me, that's where you come in.'

'You want me to look jealous,' she said doubtfully.

'I like a woman who's quick on the uptake,' he approved. 'I want you to play my classy mistress. Claw the eyes out of any woman who looks like coaxing me to dance. I don't want to fall foul of any of these financiers and annoy them by having one of their wives crawling all over me during a slow foxtrot. I have several deals in the offing and I'm damned if I'm going to risk losing those deals just because some itchy-fingered female wants to flirt.'

'I'm to protect you!' she purred in amusement.

Vigadó's eyes gleamed at her taunt. 'Call it what you like, it's the kind of thing I'm sure you do very well.'

'And the hundreds of your female fans? Couldn't you pluck one of them from your Filofax and let her gaze dreamily into your eyes all night?' She grinned.

'Other women would see it as an invitation to a relationship,' he said wryly.

'What's wrong with that?' she asked curiously.

His mouth crimped. 'I don't want the hassle.'

'You really don't like women,' she said in wonder.

'Not much. You're different. You have a businesslike attitude towards men. If they want to use you, they pay for the privilege and you all know where you are. I think perhaps you don't like men.'

Startled, she considered the idea. 'Not many,' she agreed, and suddenly felt appalled. 'Only at a distance.'

'You and I are both wary. A little cynical. That's why I can ask you to play this role and I know you won't start attaching strings to everything I do and say tonight.'

Cynical. No, she didn't want to be that! But she had been let down by men; they had turned out to be less than honourable, crashing off the pedestals she erected for them with monotonous regularity. And she'd all but given up finding a man she could really respect and love with her whole heart.

'I think I'd like to party!' She smiled, needing to cheer herself up. 'Providing my class act finishes when we leave,' she added, 'I'll do it.' He raised his glass in salute. 'I have another condition,' she said with a sweetly innocent smile. 'Usually when I do a job I prepare myself properly for it——'

'Sexy underwear—or, better still, none at all—perfumed skin——' he began huskily.

'I mean,' she said scathingly, 'that I do some research if I can. For my little role tonight, I already know who you are and what you're like—and you've explained the set-up. That's no problem. But you've given me no information about the weekend and if I'm to project the right image I'll need to know a little more about this

saga writer of yours. If there's a file on her or something, perhaps some of her work I could read, then I'd
be genned up and more likely to strike up a rapport with
her.'

She sat back, a fairly earnest expression on her face,
her hands trembling in her lap. Would he take the bait?
she wondered. If she knew for certain that it was Mary,
she could somehow get a fax to Lionel's office and book
a flight ready for a quick escape.

Vigadó appeared to be considering the idea. Coffee
arrived. Idly, he picked up a small chocolate bon-bon
and held it out to her, snatching it away when she reached
for it with her hand and obviously intending to feed her
himself. Not wanting to antagonise him, she leaned
forward and opened her mouth to receive the chocolate.

A *frisson* of excitement rampaged through her body.
The whole gesture, his ardent eyes, the thudding urgency of her heart, had all conspired to turn the gesture
into something infinitely seductive. Without taking his
eyes off hers, he picked up another sweet and slowly
brought it to her mouth again.

Every inch of her pulsated with a crazed wanting. He
leant over the table and kissed her hard on the lips and
she tasted wine and his sweet warmth as he drew her to
her feet, the kiss deepening, becoming more insistent,
till he'd nudged the table to one side and they were em-
bracing passionately, their bodies crushed together and
melding into a mindless mass of pounding rhythm as
their hearts accelerated to a breathless pace.

'Oh, you witch! I have to go,' he said with husky
regret, dropping small kisses on her lips. 'Take this
money for the dress. Get the *maître d'* to ring for a taxi.
And be in the foyer of the Hilton hotel for the party at
eight tonight.'

He'd gone before she could make her brain function.
And she realised that not only had he avoided arranging
to give her the information she'd asked for, but he'd
fooled her with kisses that she'd been alarmingly unable
to resist. A whole evening spent deliberately fawning on
him would tantalise her unbearably—and she'd be in

danger of letting him take more liberties than was wise for her.

Mariann sank into a chair. The trouble was, she had no choice but to attend the party. He was ruthless enough to dump her and choose another woman for his weekend entertainer if she irritated him.

The Hilton it would have to be. Her eyes opened, wide and startled. 'The Hilton!' she groaned. Of all places! She began to tremble. The risk of discovery was becoming greater every day. Her fear of Vigadó's potential revenge was greater, too. She had an inkling of how violent and how inventive he might be to a woman who'd strung him along. And tonight she'd have to play his mistress with dazzling conviction!

CHAPTER SEVEN

THERE was an accordion player outside the hotel. Mariann had seen him from her room earlier when she'd slipped the simple black sheath over her silky black undies. The dress was very short, very expensive and, because it had looked boring, was jazzed up considerably with the addition of hundreds of small flat bows she'd stapled to every inch of fabric.

It looked absolutely stunning, the satin ribbons shimmying with every move she made. And it was while she was shimmying in front of the mirror that she saw the white-haired old man.

He must have been freezing out there. He'd been playing for ages, his tireless, ungloved fingers rippling over the keys to produce old favourites with curlicue elaborations.

Now, as she waited for Vigadó in the foyer, she wandered over to the smoke-glass windows and watched the old man playing, his eyes closed in rapture, a permanent 'smile for the tourists' desperately stretching his lips. No one paid him any attention, and that upset her. She was about to run upstairs for a coat and some money when she saw Vigadó striding across the snow.

Mariann felt her heartbeat increase, her fingers begin to pluck nervously at the ribbons on her slender hips, where a second before she'd been supremely confident and controlled. Taken up with her irritation with herself, it was a moment before she realised that the old man was lovingly placing his accordion on a stool and fumbling awkwardly with the flip-top of a cigarette packet.

Vigadó had stopped, intently watching the old man's laboured attempts to extract a cigarette, and then to put it to his lips. Mariann wondered if he was drunk—or just numb with cold.

Several times the old man failed to light the cigarette and suddenly his strange behaviour with cupped hand and vaguely waving head made sense. He was blind! Her hands touched the glass in sudden sympathy, because passers-by swept along, unheeding, and she felt angry with them for not noticing or caring.

Except Vigadó. Quietly, he walked forward, said something graceful and polite to the man—she thought, from his gesture, he'd blamed the wind—offered a lighter and the shelter of his cupped hand and gently guided the flame to the man's cigarette.

Her body relaxed, a sweet smile on her face as she watched the scene. She felt extraordinarily touched by Vigadó's gesture. He was chatting to the man easily, making him laugh. They shook hands as friends and equals.

'I don't understand you,' breathed Mariann shakily, her palms pressing on the glass as if straining for some contact with Vigadó.

But she did know that he was hiding a lot more than he revealed. That incident had told her more than one of his guarded conversations. He felt for people. He cared. Beneath that rock-hard exterior was a soft heart and, if she read his body language with the old man correctly, a kind and generous man, too.

That fact unsettled her. Instead of feeling bright and whip-cracking smart for the evening ahead, she was on the wrong side of sentimental and dreamy! 'Wretched man!' she muttered, inwardly cursing him for spoiling her dislike of him.

He'd made one simple gesture of humanity. But because he'd thought it unobserved it had been deeply revealing of his character. Briefly she wondered whether Lionel would have stopped to light the old man's cigarette. Knowing he wouldn't made the incident harder to accept. She'd always imagined that Lionel had principles, feelings, unlike the selfish, tyrannical Vigadó.

Troubled, she moved from the window as he approached, aware that he wouldn't like her to have witnessed his kindness to the accordion player. Her huge eyes followed him as he entered and slipped off his coat to check it in at the desk. He looked devastatingly handsome, his dinner-jacket pouring over his beautiful shoulders and back like liquid silk, the trousers precision-cut, his shirt a crackling white. All eyes swivelled towards him respectfully, even those male eyes which had been glued to *her* from the moment she'd walked into the foyer.

When he saw her, he was still, as though he was about to embark on some special venture and was savouring the first moment. Her bright smile faded, their eyes meshing, passing messages across the room that somehow bypassed her brain but alerted her body. Tense, apprehensive, trembling slightly, she felt like a girl on her first date as he slowly approached.

'I kiss your hand,' he said softly, '*csókolom*!' and did so, with lingering appreciation.

And, to her confusion, she felt quite fluttery and warned herself sharply that that might be because she was a butterfly, about to have her wings broken.

'I thought you might not recognise me,' she said huskily. 'I expect you were looking for someone in black.'

His gaze dropped to her outrageously decorated dress, widened, then crinkled into a smile as he drew a chair forward and sat knee to knee with her, still retaining her hand—and unnervingly staring into her eyes like a lover.

'I hadn't registered what you were wearing, though you look fantastic,' he admitted in a velvety undertone. 'I saw your face and nothing else...' He hesitated. 'Do you think you could tell me your real name?' he asked. 'I can't call you Mimi all night.'

'Mariann,' she said huskily, taking the risk.

'Mariann.'

Stupidly, she thought when he finally said her name, drawing out the syllables in his beautifully accented brandy-rich voice, that she'd never heard it sound so beautiful before. Say it again, she urged him silently. Say it again.

'Do—do you want me to—to do or say anything special this evening?' she husked, unable to tear her eyes from his.

'No...Mariann.' Sensing her reluctant pleasure, he caressed the side of her face with the back of his hand, a light, brief gesture that caused her to lean forward, unintentionally eager for more. 'Just look into my eyes like that and everyone will know not to intrude on our territory.'

She forced her gaze downwards but he gently lifted her chin and kissed her on the mouth.

'You look very beautiful,' he murmured.

'There *is* a little black dress under this,' she said in breathy tones, trying to break away from the tension that was binding them cruelly together and somehow crushing her lungs. 'It was dull. Not me at all. I went a bit mad with a stapler——'

'Gift-wrapped yourself for me,' he smiled. 'I'm flattered.'

'No!' Had she? It had certainly taken her an eternity to get ready. Will he like this, will he like that...make-up wiped off, reapplied, brown eye-shadow, soft green, shoes everywhere, hair brushed behind the ears, feathering the face... 'I—I——'

'Touch me,' he urged, leaning closer, his mouth almost on hers. It was soft and infinitely kissable. 'Some people have come in who know me. Stroke my hair. My face. Claim me.'

She couldn't. Her limbs refused to work. Then slowly they obeyed her—with reluctance—because she knew and her body knew that once she'd touched him she'd want to pull him into her arms and kiss him till the management dragged them apart.

Tentatively her fingers brushed the short hair just behind his ears. Her light, caressing touch trailed down to the deep golden satin of his cheek and her head tipped to one side and her lips parted as her fingertips explored the change from the flawlessly smooth flesh to the hard, determined jaw.

'Oh!' she breathed, languidly draping one bare arm on his shoulder, her whole body indolent with smouldering heat.

'Don't turn round,' he murmured, nuzzling the sensitive inside of her arm with his sultry mouth. The scar on his cheek rubbed her naked shoulder, making her quiver. 'But my friends are riveted. I wish I knew...' he sighed, smiling into her lustrous eyes again. '... whether you are play-acting or your reactions are for real.'

'I'm acting, of course,' she said unsteadily. It must be Vigadó. 'I'm terribly good, aren't I, dahling?' she drawled, a little desperate to convince him.

'Alarmingly persuasive,' he said silkily. His hand ran up her long, outstretched leg, with a feather-light touch beneath her knee that convulsed her stomach. 'My problem is in working out what I feel about you.

'You don't like women. You despise me,' she said crisply. He smiled as though denying her assessment. 'I'm a call-girl you're employing, remember,' she said anxiously. 'You're reforming me.'

'I am?'

'Yes!' she insisted irritably.

'Smile at me. Caress me with your eyes,' he crooned.

She did. It came a little too easy. 'This evening is all show. Whatever it looks like to anyone else, you have to remember that I'm not going to bed with you.' She gasped when the pressure of his fingers on her stockinged thigh increased brutally. 'Vigadó!' she muttered, gritting her teeth. 'That hurts!'

'Let's go,' he said with a mocking smile. 'Dazzle the world.'

They did that, all right, he all teeth, muscular frame and impeccable manners, she fizzing with contained energy and saucy with ribbons. He kept her by his side as if they'd been welded together, introducing her to his friends and business colleagues with tenderness and lingering glances so that it must have been obvious to everyone there that they were 'deeply in love'.

She leaned against his shoulder dreamily and sipped champagne, occasionally scowling at women who spoke to Vigadó.

I'm enjoying this, she thought to her surprise. I like being with a man who's bigger, hunkier, more handsome, more commanding than any other man in the room! Her brow furrowed. Was that shallow? She shrugged. That was how she felt and there wasn't much she could do about it.

Seldom were they alone, the men talking business at every opportunity. But every now and then her eyes met Vigadó's and they were swept into a private world where the music and chatter faded into the distance and her breathing almost stopped with the overwhelming rush of feeling that consumed her body.

One of the financier's wives leaned across the table, tapping Vigadó on the hand reprovingly and breaking into one of their reveries. 'You must dance with me!' murmured the woman.

She was beautiful. Bottle-blonde, glamorous, with a cleavage that was making Vigadó blink now it was being crushed against the table and throbbing invitingly before his eyes.

'No!' snapped Mariann before he could reply. Scowling viciously, she levered the woman's immaculate fingers from where they were stroking Vigadó's hand. Her jealousy was frighteningly real.

The woman ignored her. 'Dance with me!' she husked to Vigadó.

'If he as much as touches you,' Mariann said in a low tone, 'I will make his life hell.'

'Sweetheart,' protested Vigadó. 'Helga is an old friend; her husband is——'

'Please don't!' she pleaded.

He half rose. 'I really can't——'

'I love you,' she blurted out miserably. Method acting? This was no acting! she thought as tremors shook her impassioned voice. And Vigadó's eyes had become ardent and yielding, distracting her. 'Oh, Vigadó!' She sighed as he sank in astonishment to his seat. Then she managed to pull her brain together. 'If—if you love me too, you won't want to hurt me, will you?' she said huskily.

'I don't want to, sweetheart,' he whispered, kissing her nose. 'I really don't want to.'

'Remembering your indifference to Eva, I never thought you'd be a woman's slave,' said Helga nastily, goading him to prove he wasn't.

Vigadó smiled. 'Bondage can be exciting,' he replied, keeping his eyes for the shell-shocked Mariann alone. 'Can't it?'

His light tone offered her a chance to cover up her too realistic emotions with a smokescreen. She was over-acting, nothing more.

'We love it,' she purred, while he playfully savaged her shoulder with his teeth. 'Oh, you tiger!' she admired, with a coy glance.

'I'm not sure whether to devour you or beat you,' he murmured.

'Both!' she husked, melodramatically rolling her eyes.

They laughed together, excluding the disgruntled Helga, and she felt an extraordinary bond with him. When he leaned forward to kiss her, she allowed his mouth to obliterate everyone else from her mind.

She had his permission to do this; the approval of society. Everyone could see they were an item. To the sound of indulgent chuckles, she snuggled up to Vigadó in contentment, gazing up at him in adoration. Belonging exclusively to someone suddenly seemed intensely rewarding. Loving a man like Vigadó, for instance, would be exciting—if dangerous—and for a moment or two she wanted to be his woman.

'Helga has gone,' he murmured, amusement in his eyes.

'Oh.' She drew away, disappointed.

'You're doing very well.'

'Practice,' she said lightly.

'I wonder how any man will know if you're ever speaking the truth when you tell him you love him?' he growled.

Dismayed, she dropped her eyes. They were special words, not to be casually bandied about, and she was upset that he thought she might use them in a calculating way. Even more unsettling was the fact that when she'd said she loved him the words had come welling up from her heart. Mariann sipped champagne in total bewilderment while he talked business in rapid Hungarian. Since she *didn't* love him, none of this was making sense.

He turned to her briefly. 'You're besotted with me. Pay me a little more attention.'

'Can't we have a row?' she asked hopefully.

He grinned and shook his head in exasperation. 'Don't you like being cuddled and ogled in turn?'

'Not much.'

'You're impossible!' He laughed. Then his mouth became serious. 'No wonder I'm crazy about you,' he whispered.

She wasn't ready for the tidal-wave of emotion that rushed through her. 'Ohh!' she whimpered, wishing— how *could* she?—that he weren't lying.

'Mariann.'

That sweetly spoken word didn't help. It was too tender and loving. So was the look he gave her. 'I want a row!' she said sulkily, shifting on her chair.

'I think you could do with a little physical exercise,' he murmured wickedly.

'Allow me,' murmured one of Vigadó's male acquaintances, bending close to whisper in her ear. 'You must be bored, to be so neglected. Shall we dance?'

'She dances with no one but me! No man holds her!' Vigadó rapped out.

Mariann was taken aback by his vehemence, then felt very protected, feminine and special, much to her annoyance. That was too stupid for words!

His colleague grinned and held his hands up in a placatory gesture. 'Don't blame you! But dance with her. Neglect her at your peril!'

'He's right,' Vigadó said quietly when the man had gone. 'We should dance. You've been very patient. Thank you.'

'Business is important to you, I know,' she said, trembling when he grasped her hand in his and led her to the darkened dance-floor. He turned her, put his hands on her waist and gave her a heart-stopping smile. 'I'm not exactly here to be entertained,' she said huskily.

'I have all I need now.' He pulled her against his body.

'That's good,' she said weakly, wishing she had. Then she regretted the wish, because he began the first steps in fulfilling it, his hands gently moving over her naked back where the dress dipped in a deep scoop to her waist. 'Your evening's been successful, then,' she managed, trying to make the conversation light.

'I can safely say that Dieter Ringel is well on the way to becoming a multi-national company,' he said softly. 'And, contrary to what Dieter said, I've done it without resorting to anything underhand. Thanks to you, I haven't stored up trouble for myself in the future by offending wives with my rejections. They can see I'm putty in your hands, that you'd slit my throat if I strayed. Thank you for being so convincing. I knew you could pull it off.'

Mariann wondered why she wasn't annoyed. Her whole aim in life was to bring Vigadó down, not to feel glad that she'd helped him in a small way to charm international financiers and persuade them to back his ventures. Vigadó epitomised success. Everything he touched turned to gold. Even her; she felt golden and glowing in his arms. The man was irresistible, she mused ruefully.

'Were you always sure of yourself?' she asked wryly.

'Determined,' he replied, nuzzling her ear. 'I saw what I wanted very early in life.'

'Wealth,' she said, with a faint frown.

'Everything!' he corrected her. 'I wanted everything the world had to offer. My parents were very poor, from Nyírbátor, near the Romanian and Ukraine borders. When my mother died, Father moved to Budapest to be near his sister. I was six. It was the first time I'd seen such grand, beautiful buildings and even though we were under Soviet rule there was a cosmopolitan air about

Budapest, a glamorous café society. It knocked me out.'
He smiled, his eyes soft as he remembered. 'Nyírbátor's
great claims to fame are the concerts in the Calvinist
church and its wooden bell-tower. Nothing had prepared
me for the faded decadence of this city.'

'But even in your wildest dreams,' she wondered, 'did
you ever imagine that you'd end up so rich? Do you ever
sit at your desk now and marvel that you're running a
publishing house on Castle Hill? I can't imagine how
odd it must be, to have people reading bookstand magazines and newspapers that have your own personality
and tastes stamped all over them.'

'It's not odd at all; I knew it would happen,' he said
simply. 'That's why I'm here. Because I dreamed of this
and made it come true.'

She drew her face from where it rested, cheek to cheek
with his, and leaned back a little, her expression full of
awe as they swayed to the music. 'You planned it all?'
she asked, startled.

'Everything,' he said firmly. 'I always plan, set a goal
and achieve it.'

'No failures?' Then she bit her lip, remembering the
one crucial one, his marriage. 'Sorry,' she mumbled. 'I
didn't want to hurt you.'

He stiffened. 'Whenever I've failed it's because I allowed sentiment to cloud my judgement,' he said harshly.
'It won't happen again. My plans are usually watertight.
And this...the champagne, elegant surroundings,
beautiful women...was part of my dream.'

'You set your sights high,' she said drily.

'Feet in the dirt, head in the stars,' he drawled.
'Someone has to get there. Why not me?'

'Because it was one heck of a long way for you to go,'
she mused.

'That made it an exciting challenge,' he said, his face
alive with vital energy. And she could see that his intense
desire for life had carried him onwards and upwards. 'I
used to walk to the waterfront on the Pest side of the
river and look up at Castle Hill with its palace, its church
where our kings were crowned, its symbols of power and

wealth. I'd tell myself that only a strip of water sep-
arated me from my dream to be up there, drinking coffee
with the diplomats and wealthy foreigners—and that
there was a bridge across that water.'

'The Chain Bridge,' she breathed, marvelling at how
clearly he'd seen his fairy-tale future—and had made it
real.

'Széchenyi Iánchid.' He smiled in agreement. 'It
seemed to me that merely by putting one foot in front
of the other I could walk over the bridge and come closer
to my goal. All that was left after that was to climb the
hill. I had to decide whether to take the fast route or the
slow one.'

She thought of his marriage which had taken him directly to the top at the tender age of—what would it
have been?—eighteen? 'You mean the slow, hard slog
on foot from the Watertown, or the more rapid ascent
by the funicular,' she said soberly. 'You chose the fast
route.'

'You think I cheated? Some people think I was clever.'

'I think you were calculating,' she said huskily. 'Cold-
blooded.' But she had to admit that, even if he'd married
Eva for who she was, he'd grown to love her—and been
punished by losing that love. Fate had a way of evening
things out, she mused wryly.

His eyes were clouded when they met hers. 'How old
are you?'

'Twenty-three.'

'I was divorced by your age,' he muttered. 'Married
before my soul was fully developed,' he added, his mouth
curling with cynicism.

'Do you regret that now?' she asked hesitantly. If he
said yes, she could begin to respect him. If the answer
was no, then she must steel her heart and remember that
they were enemies, whatever her body kept telling her.

'Yes and no,' he said, confounding her. 'I have the
success I wanted. I've known happiness.'

'But?' she prompted.

'But there's a price. I don't want you to make my mis-
takes, Mariann.'

'Why?' she asked shakily.

'Because inside that sophisticated, worldly woman I can see a tender-hearted girl who's a long way from her origins and has come too far, too fast. If you have dreams, consider carefully how you intend to fulfil them.' His eyes were serious and compassionate, haunting her with their longing. 'You see, if you decide to travel fast, by funicular, you're locked in. It becomes a cage. Sure, you rise quickly—but you can't stop to take in your surroundings at your leisure, and you look out from a restricted viewpoint.'

Her heart was beating rapidly, at precisely the same rate as his. In fact they seemed bound together, their bodies fitting as if they'd been fashioned for each other and no one else.

'You're saying that with hindsight it would have been better if you'd had a longer struggle for success,' she said, controlling the shake in her voice with difficulty, 'and perhaps enjoyed the achievement more. Although, whichever way you went, you would have got to the top just the same,' she observed sadly, wishing he'd never abandoned all his principles.

'Of course,' he said, with quiet confidence. In the subdued light of the flickering candles, his skin looked as if it had been painted with gold. But there was pain in the lines around his eyes and mouth and a bitterness on his lips that made her think of King Midas, who'd wished for riches and had lost everything he loved in the process. 'It's too late to change what happened in my life,' he said softly. 'But not too late for you.'

'What do you mean?' she muttered warily.

'You're young, ambitious, with a streak of ruthlessness,' he murmured. His finger lightly toyed with a strand of her chestnut hair. 'Think over what you want in life very carefully. Be prepared to change your mind about the people you've worked for. Remember that the only person who cares about your welfare is you, your family, and...the man who will be your lover. Everyone else is working for their own interests. You've sold yourself, Mariann. Sold yourself short. You're worthy of greater things than those you've become involved in.'

Her stricken eyes searched his, a rush of tenderness sweeping through her. Perhaps he was showing concern because he thought they'd both chosen dubious means to get rich. Maybe he wanted her to avoid the emptiness he'd discovered in his life, the ruined marriage, the bitter realisation that it wasn't how successful you were that counted, only how you lived.

'You know I'm turning over a new leaf,' she said, incredibly wishing she could make his life happier. Madness. Sheer madness.

'But at the moment you're only paying lip-service to the idea,' he said quietly. 'You haven't really understood what I'm driving at. Make sure that you think long and hard about your boss and how he's used you.'

Vigadó drew her close again, pressing her head into his shoulder, and gently steered her around the dance-floor. And this time she did think, but not of some non-existent boss of a call-girl racket. She thought of Lionel. How he'd used her for his own needs, how she'd soft-heartedly agreed to help and landed herself in trouble while Lionel disappeared and waited to be handed the information he wanted on a plate. This wasn't what she wanted in life—deceiving a man who was tough and competitive but who probably had given Mary O'Brien a better deal than she was getting from Lionel.

She heaved a deep sigh. Warm lips touched her forehead. 'I need to talk to you,' he whispered.

'Talk,' she mumbled in strangled tones.

'Not here. My flat.'

Her loins contracted. 'No,' she breathed, overcome by the longing.

'I have to be there,' he said huskily. 'I need privacy. It's about Eva. And it's about you.'

'Vigadó——' she began. But he played unfairly again, kissing her so sweetly that all she could do was to cling to him in helpless delight as his mouth tenderly moved over hers, lulling her senses, rendering her mind quite defenceless and trusting.

He led her out of the room and she glided along beside him as if on auto-pilot. 'My coat,' he said to the woman behind the desk and handing her a ticket. 'Yours?' he asked Mariann.

'Oh! I—I didn't have one.' She cursed herself for not bringing one down.

'You came in just that?' he asked in gentle amazement.

'Taxis are warm,' she defended miserably. 'Look, I don't think I should——'

'You want to know about your author, don't you?' he said, draping his soft coat around her shoulders and smilingly cuddling her. 'Her background, her address, that kind of thing?'

Even more miserable, she nodded dumbly. But she didn't think she wanted to do this any more. It seemed like betraying a friend. But this had gone too far for her to back out.

'You won't—you...' She tried again. 'You say you want me to change my way of life,' she croaked, distressed by the warmth in his eyes. She hated deceiving him now. Oh, heavens! Was she going crazy? 'Vigadó, you must understand that I have to learn to respect myself.' Her voice shook. Clearing her throat, she slicked her tongue over her lips, wishing he wouldn't smile so beguilingly at her with such trust and hope in his eyes. 'I don't think you and I...that we should...should become in—in...' She couldn't say it. Her embarrassment was total.

'Intimate. I know. I can't expect you to stop letting men use you, and then use you myself,' he provided huskily.

'That's right,' she said in relief. Then thought with honesty that only part of her was relieved.

'OK,' he said, escorting her to the door. 'Would you rather cancel this weekend?'

'No!' she said sharply, then frowned. 'I don't know,' she admitted. 'I'm not normally confused, but——'

'Come back with me,' he coaxed. 'I'll explain what I'd like you to do this weekend and you can decide then and there if you want to escort this author or leave her to me.' He tucked her more firmly into the coat and she realised they were already outside. 'I can't pretend I don't want you,' he said huskily. 'But there are certain things I'm prepared to wait for. I've made a mess of my relationship with Eva. I don't want to ruin this too.'

'What . . . do you mean?' she whispered.

He smiled at her upturned face. 'I mean that I'd rather walk slowly with you than race ahead. It's more exciting, more tantalising. And I'm going to get there, anyway.'

'Get where?' she said thickly.

'That mouth of yours would melt icicles,' he murmured.

'It might need to, if we stay here any longer,' she mumbled, annoyed that he hadn't answered her directly.

Vigadó laughed. 'We could have a snowfight and warm up!'

'In this dress, these shoes?' she cried, waving one spindly-heeled shoe in front of her. 'I can hardly walk in these conditions, let alone dash about the snow dodging your lethal aim.'

'I am a bit underhand, aren't I?' he said smugly.

'Yes. But I'll get my own back one day!'

'I don't think you will,' he said.

And something faintly sinister in the softly spoken words made her examine his face anxiously but he just smiled and averted his head. 'They've cleared a path,' he continued in a distant tone. 'We'll take the more roundabout route and save your shoes, at least, from ruination.'

She held on to him firmly, afraid she'd slip. He must have been cold, because his body was tense, but he didn't shiver and she had the impression that he was willing himself not to.

A nameless fear began to make her pulses race. She couldn't really trust him—it would be foolish to do so. 'Vigadó,' she said with as much decisiveness as she could muster, 'if you want to talk to me in private, then we can do that in your office just as well as your apartment.'

'Fine by me.' She blinked, disconcerted by his easy agreement. Perhaps she'd been maligning his intentions. 'I'll find the janitor and let him know we're in here. You turn up the heating in my office and make yourself comfortable—perhaps put the coffee on. There's something I want to fetch from my apartment and I have to check my phone calls.' He unhooked the flat key from the ring and handed the rest of the keys to her. 'Let yourself in; I'll try not to keep you waiting but I haven't had time to play back the calls that have been made from the flat.'

Astounded, and only half listening to what he was saying, she stared at the huge bunch of keys in her hand, turning them over. They would unlock everything. Including the filing cabinet in his room that she knew held authors' files.

'What are you thinking, Mariann?' he asked softly.

She forced a smile while her brain whipped up a good answer. 'There are so many of these, they must ruin your expensive suits!' she cracked quickly.

He turned abruptly as though her answer had disturbed the cosy atmosphere and then strode towards the lighted room where the night janitor sat.

Mariann knew she didn't have much time. With trembling fingers, she found the right keys to unlock the side-doors, the inner doors and then, finally, the one to his office. Without switching on the light, she hurried to the filing cabinet and went through all the small keys till one of them turned in the lock.

She pulled out the top drawer. Her fingers located the 'O's.

'I forgot to say,' came his low drawl. Mariann whirled around and gave a little choking cry as the light snapped on. 'Don't be afraid,' he said, coming to slam his hands on either side of her, holding the drawer open. 'It's only me.' His eyes gleamed malevolently. 'I came to tell you where I hid the decent coffee.' His eyes scanned her white face. 'Nothing to be afraid of, is there?'

'You gave me a shock! I wasn't...'

'Expecting me?' he murmured. 'Why are you looking in my files, Mariann?'

She gulped, her eyes huge with anxiety. 'I wondered where you kept the coffee,' she said lamely. 'I thought under "C"...'

'Or you were looking for information about a certain British author.'

Mariann's body froze. She stared up at him while her stomach contracted in fear. He knew. He knew everything.

CHAPTER EIGHT

SMILING faintly, Vigadó lifted a dark eyebrow. 'Isn't that right? You're keen to do a little advance homework. You wanted to get genned up, didn't you?' he queried, moving away and setting up the espresso machine. 'You thought I might forget to tell you. And you like to know everything about people you are employed to entertain, don't you?'

She was saved! She gave a trembly smile. 'Uh-huh,' she agreed, nodding to reinforce her croaky voice.

'You'll know all about her, I promise,' he said. 'But I want to tell you something more important first.' Pushing the cabinet door shut, he held out his hand for the keys and then pocketed them. She'd missed her opportunity and made him wary. Mentally she kicked herself, hard, several times. 'Watch the coffee-machine while I go upstairs a moment. Won't be long. Mine's black. No sugar.'

Despite the fact that her legs shook so much that she wobbled perilously on her spindly shoes, Mariann managed to cross the room when he'd gone, to turn up the central heating, and then gratefully sank into a deep leather armchair by the desk. She wasn't sure if she'd made him suspicious or not. However, she didn't want to believe that he was. If he suspected her, she knew he'd keep his suspicions to himself but wreak some awful revenge.

So she put herself in a state of limbo, refusing to consider that she was in danger. It was the only thing that stopped her from running away. By disappearing, she'd turn any suspicions he might have into certainties. Bluff it out, she told herself. Make him laugh. She could do it.

138

At least she had time to compose herself. He'd take a while, checking through his phone calls... Her eyes bolted open. 'Phone calls!' she gasped. Did he mean that calls from the flat were monitored? She licked her dry lips. Who had she rung? What had she said?

Her father. That had been the normal chat of a daughter who cared, a father who was happily enjoying life. Sue. She'd rung Sue. Nothing incriminating there, other than the fact that she and her younger sister missed one another and their father was thriving.

She went pink. The 'madam' at the London number! In order to discover the truth, she'd pretended to be one of the 'girls', ringing in to say that the job was taking a little longer than expected! Still, that fitted in with Vigadó's picture of her.

'Oh, what a tangled web!' she groaned. The next half-hour could be crucial.

'Coffee's ready,' she trilled, hearing him come in while she was placing the cups on their saucers.

'Thanks,' he said tersely.

The cups in her hand wobbled and she put them down before the whole lot spilt. 'You look annoyed. Nasty messages from your bank manager?' she sympathised brightly, deciding to go on the attack.

The muscles of his jaw shifted beneath the taut skin. 'You made a lot of calls,' he said softly.

She jumped as though someone had put electrodes to her skin and he pulled her roughly to him, his eyes accusing, pitch-dark pools that were making her sway like a drunken fool on the edge of an abyss.

'Women chatter.' She sighed, with a sweet, blinking look.

'And men react,' he said tightly.

She felt herself tremble. 'Don't be mean,' she chided in desperation. 'You can afford a few calls.'

'You'll pay for them,' he muttered, with an unnervingly sinister tone in his voice.

'I've just done you a favour, defending you from the ruthless Helga,' she said defiantly, 'and all you can do is complain about your phone bill!'

He gazed at her steadily and then released her. 'Yes,' he growled. 'You have done me a favour. Thank you.'

Her breath rushed out in pure relief. 'It was fun,' she retorted more cheerfully, hardly able to believe that she'd escaped discovery. He can't have listened very carefully. Or perhaps the device only recorded the number of calls, not the conversations. She felt her muscles ease. 'I think you rather enjoyed it, too.'

'I'm afraid I did.' He smiled thinly. 'Which is why I want you to have a look at this.'

He handed over what she knew to be the photograph of Eva. She sat down, crossing her long, dark-stockinged legs and glanced at it quickly. 'Your ex-wife.'

'And?'

Frowning, she looked again. In the background, dimly and almost as an afterthought, was a child. Vigadó's child. Mariann knew that immediately. She had his dark eyes, the selfsame stubborn, uncompromisingly sour expression for the càmera. 'Your daughter?' she asked quietly, her mind whirling.

'Lindi.' He sank into the chair behind his desk and sipped the hot coffee, his eyes lowered. 'She was the reason I stayed close to Eva. She was the one I loved, the one I will miss, whose memories I have to forget or be destroyed.'

Mariann was astounded. 'Are you telling me that you weren't upset at losing your wife?' she asked in amazement.

'Correct.' He leaned back, scowling at the neat crease in his trousers. 'I didn't love Eva. I never did.'

'Yet you married her!' she gasped.

'Yes,' he growled, offering no reason, no excuse. 'When Lindi came along, I was touched by love for the first time. Eva hated to see me with Lindi, loving her, adoring her, doing things for her...' He gritted his teeth, forcing some control over his emotions. 'Her revenge was to alienate Lindi from me till our house became a battleground and Lindi was in danger of being torn in two.'

'So you left,' she said gently.

'I had no choice. She would have destroyed her own daughter to punish me. I don't think Eva knows how to love, only to possess. I forced Eva to divorce me. Black or white, you see. I loathe half-measures. And she promised access on the understanding that I kept the divorce a secret.' He exhaled a long, deep sigh. 'I thought I'd be able to handle being a part-time father.'

'But you couldn't,' Mariann prompted, her heart illogically torn for him.

'It was vile. I decided I'd prefer a clean break rather than a ragged, painful wound,' he said harshly. 'Making plans to see Lindi and then having them thwarted was eating me up——'

'I see!' she exclaimed. 'When you talked about broken appointments, birthday presents returned, you meant that Eva had stopped you seeing Lindi,' she said in sudden understanding. 'And that hurt you so much, so often, that you wanted to get out of that hell and try to live without either of them.'

'Exactly.'

Mariann wondered why she felt relieved. He didn't love his ex-wife. He'd adored his daughter and had suffered from Eva's cruel revenge. She should feel pity for him—but not relief, or this destructive warm affection.

'I'm sorry.' She sighed. 'But can't you insist? How old is Lindi?'

'Eight.'

She leant forward. 'But...she can't be! You're twenty-six!' Her face coloured at his shrewd, assessing glance. 'Someone said,' she muttered in explanation.

'Really,' he said drily.

'You were young when you met her,' she said.

'Yes. I was hanging around outside the big hotels, hoping to earn some spare money guiding tourists. I was eighteen, she was twenty-two, with a mind of her own and rebellion in her eyes. I took her around Budapest. She showed me the inside of her room, then her bed, and gave me a private tour of her body. And she followed me like a faithful dog for the two months that

Dieter spent here, setting up his first Hungarian branch of his business.'

'You didn't love her,' she said, faintly disapproving.

'People have sex without love, as you are all too well aware,' he said coldly. 'She gave me an insight into the life I wanted. I learnt how to behave in smart hotels, elegant restaurants, how to choose wine. I was dazzled.'

'And she became pregnant,' Mariann said quietly.

'She made sure of that,' he replied, his face grim. 'She insisted we get married. Dieter was aghast, but she threatened to run away and he loved his daughter above everything. So he decided to groom me for stardom. I had a duty to Eva. She was carrying my child. It seemed my reward for a loveless marriage was to be the life I'd always dreamed of. It seemed a fair exchange at the time. And here I am.'

Cold. Unemotional. Mariann shivered. 'What happened to happiness on the way?' she asked huskily.

'I'm working on that.' The hypnotic darkness of his eyes deepened. 'I think I've found the one woman who could make me forget.'

Her cup rattled again in her hand and she put it on the desk without taking her eyes off him. 'Vigadó...'

'Come here,' he ordered softly. 'What I have to say is too personal to be spoken across a desk.'

'I thought you mocked my agony-aunt role,' she said, venturing a weak joke at her own expense.

He held his hand out. 'Come.' And, like a fool, driven by some unconscious need, she obeyed. 'Whatever I think of your role,' he said, pulling her unresisting body between his knees, 'I can't deny that you have a dramatic effect on my libido.'

'Don't think you can use sex to help you forget you were ever a father,' she muttered angrily. Her arms kept them at a decent distance. His hands were already sliding up her legs, pushing up the hem of her skirt, and the hunger in his face was driving her insane with an unwilling, unwanted desire.

'No. It won't,' he said shortly.

'You said you didn't want to use me——'

'I don't.' His fingers touched the tops of her black stockings and his breath hissed in as he explored the satin suspender belt. 'But sex—you—can make me a man again.'

Bewildered, Mariann stared without making sense of what he'd said. Make him a man? He *was* a man—far too much of him was all male, all conquering...

He kissed her, deep and hard and fast, his lips driving into hers till she felt the pressure of his teeth behind them. Swaying on her feet, she struggled and moaned, dismayed that he'd betrayed his promise to leave her alone. He'd said he wouldn't rush at her; he'd given her to understand that he wasn't intending to seduce her. And she'd fallen for his ploy.

'No!' she said fiercely, snatching her mouth away.

'For the first time,' he growled, 'in six years I've wanted a woman. For all that time I've been impotent— till you came along with your saucy body and provocative smile, the sway of your hips, the wickedness in your eyes, and my desire leapt into life as if it had never known such temptation.'

'You?' she gasped. 'You?'

'Laugh and I'll kill you,' he snarled savagely, his eyes black with violence. 'Can you have any idea what that's done to me? To be a husband who can't make love to his wife? To seem to be the height of savage manhood to dozens of women and yet not feel the slightest stirrings of desire?'

'Oh, God!' she whispered. Her hands touched his hair, his furrowed forehead, the deep crease between the eyebrows.

'This is why Eva has always shrugged off claims by other women. She knew that my anger with life was directed at myself. And as long as that lasted she also knew that I was still impotent. Until she saw you and me together.'

Mariann thought of Lionel's assertion that Vigadó was promiscuous. Gossip, nothing more. What else was hearsay? she wondered. 'Vigadó... you're putting a lot of trust in me by telling me this,' she said shakily.

'I need you,' he muttered roughly. His head rested against her pelvis and she felt his hands exploring higher, the soft silk of her thighs melting into his eager caresses as though surrendering. She gave an inarticulate cry and he held her more tightly. 'I need you so badly, Mariann,' he murmured. 'I've been in a state of unrelieved desire ever since we met. I want you. If that had been all, I would have taken you long ago. But there's more.'

He stood up, lifting her dress to her waist as he did so, his eyes dominating her, paralysing her while he caught her fiercely to him, his fingers splaying over the satin of her small briefs and exploring the warm softness of her bottom.

'More?' she mumbled into his mouth, unconsciously offering its moist interior to him. She flinched, savouring the sinful thrust of his tongue, giving herself for a fraction of a second to the wonderful wantonness that lay inside her.

It was enough. She heard his hand sweep across his desk, clearing it, and then she was being lifted, her back contacting the hard surface and Vigadó had covered her with his hot, hard body.

And, hot and hard, his desire stirred against her thin triangle of satin while his mouth savaged her shoulders, her throat, her breasts...

They were naked! 'How did you get to my—my——?'

'Does it matter?' he said thickly, touching each breast with such wonder and delight that she felt a devastating ripple of pride and joy that he should find her beautiful and desirable.

'No.'

It didn't matter, she thought. It was too late for how or why. Both of them knew she wanted this, that she had hungered for him from the very beginning. It didn't have to make sense. Sexual chemistry had no logic. They were dynamite together; it was as simple and as complex as that.

'Mariann!' He spoke her name with poetic ardour and she quivered from head to toe. 'I will unwrap my present,' he said huskily, reaching down beneath and sliding down the zip. 'Layer by layer.' In a quick movement, the dress was whisked from her body and he was studying—no, virtually worshipping, she realised, with a heart-tugging pleasure—the sensual curves of her breasts, the tingling, painful nipples that felt as though they were leaping towards him eagerly.

She moaned and innocently writhed to try and ease the terrible ache that fired the core of her body. 'We have to stop,' she said with difficulty.

'You can't do that to me,' he muttered, his eyes glittering. 'You know you can't.'

'Not here,' she protested weakly, playing for time. Perhaps she'd come to her senses if she could have a moment to think, without his touch. 'Oh!' she gasped, clutching his head tightly.

He had bent forward, lifted one breast to his mouth and sucked. It felt as though she'd been switched on, the hot blood in her body rushing like a released dam towards that one focus—the empty womanhood that he wanted so badly.

'Yes,' he groaned. 'Here. Now. And then anywhere you choose. Everywhere. All night long,' he rasped. 'In pain?' he muttered, seeing the anguished hunger in her face.

Yes, she wanted to say. One breast is starving for your mouth. He ripped off his jacket, tore away his tie and she began to feel afraid. If she wanted to stop him, it had to be now. If.

'Slowly,' she said, her throat refusing to let her speak clearly. It sounded as though she was drunk. Perhaps she was—drunk with desire, with the intoxication of too frequent sips of his potent masculinity. 'You said...*slowly*.'

'Your eyes are drugged,' he whispered hoarsely. 'You find this as exciting as I do—and I want you too much to be slow. Slow can come later.' His shirt was yanked from his body in a quick, urgent gesture. 'You'll understand. I have six years of desire waiting to be shared with you. I know how men must have treated you in the past.

This won't be anything like that. No weird practices,'
he growled, his hand undoing her suspenders. 'Only a
long, lusty night of sex with a man driven insane by
desire.'

Delicately, he rolled down one stocking and then the
other, while Mariann let him. He thought she was used
to this, that she could take a man's passion and be none
the worse for it. Her eyes closed and then her whole
body arched with shock as an incredible sensation ran
through it.

'Vigadó!' she croaked, panting, struggling for breath.
It came again, a profoundly deep rippling explosion that
sent the blood roaring in her head and a shame that he
was touching her...*there*. Her hand covered his, her eyes
pleading.

Ruthlessly, he held her gaze and continued to rub
gently. Her eyes began to close as the spasms took over
the whole of her existence. There was the sound of
tearing and she realised he'd ripped her briefs into pieces.

'I will have you,' he said savagely. 'Even if it's at the
cost of my heart and my soul. Touch me!' he demanded.

She stared, shaking. 'Heart? Soul?' she repeated
stupidly.

'I said there was more,' he breathed, taking her hand
and kissing it. Then he pressed it against the hard swelling
of his body and it leapt beneath her palm, making her
draw in a shuddering breath. 'I'm in great danger,
Mariann,' he whispered. 'I may be falling in love with
you.'

A kick of tender desire jolted her heart, letting it pour
into the melting-pot that was her surrendering body. And
her brain followed. 'Love?' she breathed. 'You can't—
I don't——'

'No one's asking you. Pretend this is another job. Help
me. Look into that tender heart of yours and help me
out of my hell. I need you. Deeply, desperately, madly.
And you, you are so beautiful, the perfect combination
of virgin and whore. Wicked, sensual, tempting,
emotional, fragile, compassionate. How can you say no?'

he murmured, his passionate kisses trailing hot fire all over her body.

Love.

And she was weak, distracted by his revelation, defenceless now against his kisses, the sweet agony his fingers were causing. Her mind, her own heart, her own soul—all had been skilfully besieged, captured, tamed…

'No,' she moaned. 'No.'

'Too late,' he growled. 'Far, far too late.'

She jerked, groaning with the onslaught of his mouth, the adoring words, the worship of her body. Faster and faster her breath came, deeper and deeper she sank in a world of sensual abandon, longing for such a man who would love her, bring her passion and desire, match her strength and be her lover.

His own rapid breathing rasped in her ear. She felt her hands being stretched over her head and he was looking down on her naked, defenceless body, his eyes glittering with a strange light. One knee thrust her legs apart. Still he gazed at her, his muscles tensed like whipcords.

And, shameful hussy that she was, she silently begged for him, despairing of herself and incapable of imagining what she would do afterwards, but knowing that nothing other than Vigadó's lovemaking could ever ease the compelling need she had to be part of him. Her madness told her she loved him and she wanted to believe that, if only to excuse her wanton behaviour.

Love.

He smiled and her heart leapt. His eyes softened and her body flowed for him. 'Yes, Vigadó,' she said huskily, 'Yes, yes, yes, *please!*'

Mariann's gasping cry at her loss of virginity went unheard, drowned by Vigadó's raw, primitive groan of need as he filled her. Their bodies meshed, tangled, fought fiercely for release and she felt that her pain and pleasure would make her die, that she couldn't stay sane and know such wonderful torment. Whimpering, pleading, moaning, she felt the full force of Vigadó's unchained passion.

And somewhere in the back of her mind she wondered if she would ever be able to meet her own eyes in a mirror again.

'You bitch!' he muttered thickly, ravishing her mouth with a shockingly elemental ferocity. 'You bitch! God, I could...I could... Hell and damnation!' he whispered hoarsely. 'I want you so *badly*!'

'Don't hurt me!' she pleaded, suddenly frightened. What had she *done*?

But she saw the predatory hunger in his face and knew he had waited too long for a woman. She struggled and they fell heavily to the floor, rolling over and over, crashing into furniture, a table, scrambling on to a chair, and all the time she was wrapping her legs around his strong body, revelling in the beauty of his muscled flesh, the touch of warm satin skin, the sheer animal maleness of him.

Horrified. Elated. Lusting after him. She groaned.

With brutal gentleness, he lapped at her breast and slowly began to move within her. Mariann threw her head back in wild delight, unable to hide how wonderful it was, aching from the heart-wrenching rapture on his face.

'Mariann,' he mumbled thickly. 'Sweet girl...wild woman...my dream come true.'

'Ohh!' she moaned, half hysterical with the throbbing power that claimed her body. She was frightened, really frightened of the power that those words had on her. And something else. Instinct told her that his despair was not born of a hatred of her, but because he was fighting the strange, intangible chains that bound them together.

A flash of insight seared through her mind. Without the forces that were keeping them apart, they would be soul-mates. She knew it with a conviction that hurt because they could never find happiness together; too much was between them.

'I hate you for making me feel like this!' he hissed.

Yet his kiss was tender, cruelly so, and suddenly she was shouting out, 'Vigadó, please, please don't hurt me; I love you, I love you!'

She was picked up bodily. Pushed to a wall. Pictures, ornaments fell around her and she opened her eyes wide to see that his were filled with savagery and a devil brooded in his face.

'Evil witch!' he kept saying, desperately, unhappily, with every relentless thrust of his body.

She knew that he mistakenly hated her for being a woman of easy virtue. That he loathed himself for needing her. And her heart went out to him even more. Why couldn't they love? she thought resentfully. Why wouldn't he allow himself to take that risk?

'Love me,' she said, hardly aware that she did. 'Love me, Vigadó!'

'I won't!' he grated jerkily. 'I—oh, God, Mariann!'

They fell on to cushions while the world began to spin dizzily and everything in her body turned into fire for him. I love him, she thought helplessly. Then his mouth drowned out all thought, all knowledge of reality, and the ecstasy captured her and made her a prisoner for ever.

Exhausted, she mumbled and muttered small, breathless words and lay supine in his arms. Silently, grimly even, he stroked her shaking body, his eyes wide open and staring at the ceiling. Then he leaned over and began to kiss her, raising her to a passion again and lifting her with cruelly mocking eyes to the desk.

There must have been a night, there must have been a morning, but she was unaware of either. Vigadó's stamina was awesome. And every time, though she felt she would never move, breathe, let alone respond once more, he touched her with such an electrifying sensuality that she found herself begging for him yet again, and again, and again...

Beneath his sleeping body, she heard the sounds of the city. For the moment she needed to lie still and let her mind return to normal. There was nothing she could do about her body. Last night it hadn't belonged to her at all, but to the whore she'd impersonated.

Mariann felt her skin heat up with the deep blush that coloured it. She'd never known people could behave like that. There had been no violence, none of the dark sexual practices she'd feared. Passion, yes, the passion and ecstasy that she'd dreamed of. He'd worshipped her with his body and his eyes and even now she felt weak at the memory and a wonderful rapture stirred her heart.

Vigadó had taught her where to touch him, and she'd become bolder as the hours went by, exhilarated by the intoxicating power of sexual love... She blushed more furiously, refusing to admit to herself the enjoyment she'd known under his hands.

That one man could give so much pleasure...!

She had to get away. It was an episode she must conceal from herself—or she would be admitting that she liked to run with the devil. What they'd done had been sinful...

Her body leapt into life and she squeezed her thighs together tightly, deeply distressed that he now possessed her, body, heart and soul. A sickness clawed at her stomach. 'Oh, my God!' she whispered. She'd said he'd never be able to destroy her heart and soul—and he had! Her hands shook. Had he done that deliberately?

With frantic fear making her nerves jerk her weary body into life, she began to ease herself from his enclosing arms. Slowly, delicately, her breath held in an agony of suspense, she managed it without waking him. When she looked down, he looked so serene that she wanted to bend and kiss his softly parted lips. Instead she gritted her teeth. She'd dress and leave, make light of what had happened and... She gasped.

The room had been wrecked. Mariann's eyes opened wide. 'No, no!' she husked miserably, refusing to accept that she had lain on that desk, invited him with seductively enticing gestures to make love to her; that she'd explored his body and knew every inch... She covered her face in horror.

The shame. The terrible, sickening shame! All her principles, her morality, her father—dear heaven, her *father*!

Fury rippled through her. Against Lionel, for getting her into this situation; Vigadó for taking advantage of her; and her own stupid, weak hunger for a man who seemed to be made of iron and yet had needed her. It had been a heady flattery and one that she'd been unable to resist.

Her hands stilled on the desk clock and calendar. Saturday. Two in the afternoon! Mary would have been waiting for them somewhere, perhaps given up and gone back to her hotel. Maybe the Hilton. She'd find out. If Vigadó had meant this episode to divert her from her real purpose, he'd misjudged the strength of her determination. Meanwhile, there was something else she could do: find that file and leave with it.

She located her briefs but they'd been ripped to shreds. Her dress was reasonably preserved. Shivering with the cold, since the central heating wasn't operating, she wriggled into the dress then slipped her arms into his vicuña coat and felt instantly warmer.

With a wary backward glance at Vigadó's sleeping form, she picked up the keys from amid the chaotic muddle of papers and contents of Vigadó's attaché case that spilled on to the floor. She froze, her eyes glued to a typescript half in, half out of the case. Tentatively her hand eased it out a little further. The words on the frontispiece leapt up at her: 'Daughters of Ireland'...her eyes flicked down the page ' . . . by Mary O'Brien.'

Her trembling fingers picked it up. There was an address on the front. Visegrád! What was she doing there? She knew it! It lay on the Danube, to the west of Budapest! And yet Mary was supposed to be coming from Heathrow. Maybe she'd made a trip to see Liz and had been working all this time in a secret Hungarian location.

Her breath hurting her chest, she slipped on her shoes, but instead of hurrying out she quickly flipped open the typescript to read the first line.

And was hooked. It was different from anything Mary had written before. More powerful. Feverishly she turned over, reading rapidly. A masterpiece! No wonder there had been a tussle for it. This would break all records!

'It's irresistible, isn't it?' said Vigadó softly.

She jumped in dismay. Her eyes slanted in his direction. He had levered himself up on one elbow and was watching her intently. 'Stunning. I can't bear to put it down,' she said honestly. 'Can I take it and read it?' she asked as casually as she could.

'Is that what you were going to do?' he asked menacingly. 'Walk out and leave me, taking some reading matter with you?'

'I—I was afraid to face you,' she said in a low tone, with perfect truth.

'Put the typescript down, Mariann,' he ordered. 'It's not leaving this office. And nor are you.'

Her eyes grew apprehensive. 'Why?' she asked, regretfully placing Mary's masterpiece on the desk.

'After last night? This morning? Look what we did to this room! Is that chaos or isn't it?' he asked in mocking amusement.

Red to the roots of her hair, she nodded stiffly. 'I'll help to tidy up——'

'No!' He chuckled, lazily standing, quite unperturbed about his nudity. 'Don't you know that this room echoes what's inside my head at the moment? Isn't your mind messed about, too?'

'The sex was good,' she said, trying to sound as if she had something—someone—to compare it with.

'Good?' His eyes narrowed and he walked towards her, his eyes full of a dark intent. 'You know very well that it wasn't "good".'

'It wasn't?' she gaped indignantly.

'No. It was explosive, ecstatic, exquisite, all-consuming,' he said, laughing triumphantly to see the exhilaration roar through her with the fevered memories. 'Even allowing for my delight in discovering I was a normal, healthy male again, I have to admit that it was tender and sweet and emotional too and that you reached parts of me I never knew existed.' He grimaced. 'And you were only doing your job.'

'What do you mean?' she asked warily.

'Please, no more denials,' he muttered. 'I think I should tell you that I have confirmation of your identity.'

'What?' She gasped, the colour draining from her face.

'You betrayed yourself on the phone. I am certain that you've been hired to take Mary O'Brien away from me.'

Nerves clawed at her stomach. He'd known—and yet he hadn't brutalised her; on the contrary. 'What—what are you going to do?' she asked in a low whisper.

'I've begun already.'

She didn't understand his reaction at all. Though...he'd said 'hired'. Mercifully, it seemed that he knew nothing of her true relationship with Lionel— or she might not have still been in one piece. But he knew she'd duped him, and why. Her eyes implored him to understand her torn loyalties.

'I didn't like deceiving you,' she said miserably.

'We've both been deceitful,' he drawled. 'I set out to seduce you from the moment we met.' Her eyes widened and his mouth twisted in a self-mocking smile. 'I wanted you. I wanted that...life, that vitality. It hadn't occurred to me that once I'd had you I'd want to move heaven and earth to keep you. Stay. Stay for me.'

Mariann trembled at the steely determination in his glittering eyes. 'No! No more... I—I'd better go,' she whispered, unable to make her feet move an inch. They wanted to stay; the whole of her wanted to stay!

'Why? Because you're afraid of becoming sexually involved with your client's enemy?' he suggested grimly.

She lifted her chin high. 'Something like that.'

'But you are involved. We know each other; after last night, I know your body by heart,' he murmured remorselessly. 'My lips and fingers have learnt every inch of you and I have taught you what I like. We please each other, Mariann. Why waste good sex?'

'I can't stay! It's impossible!' she rasped.

'Is it?' he asked softly. 'Think about what you want and how you will get it.'

Mariann stared at him, stricken. She wanted him. All she had to do was to reach out. But the consequences of that action would be too great. He'd own her, possess her mind and her body, suffocating her till she was a mere toy for him to play with. She feared the great well of love that lay waiting to be tapped inside her, knowing that if she did surrender to a man as ruthless and calculating as Vigadó she would be terribly vulnerable. Slavery wasn't her idea of a relationship. She would love him too much and he wouldn't care at all. Any whore could do what she'd just done for him.

'I—can't... I'm appalled at what we did... I've never behaved like that before,' she admitted miserably.

'Life can be a bitch, can't it?' he said with a savage softness. 'Ruining our well-planned lives. But I think we'd both be mad to walk away from each other and deny how much pleasure we've had. Why not stay and have fun?' he suggested more lightly. 'No commitments, no ties.'

'You... you want me to stay, even when you know all about me?' she began jerkily.

'It doesn't matter to me that you're a call-girl,' he muttered, destroying her theory that he had despised himself for wanting her. So why had he been so angry? Perhaps, she mused, he just didn't like losing control. Unsure where that left her, she watched him begin to dress. 'Or that you're trying to get information back to the man who hired you—and you know who that is,' he growled, 'despite pretending to the contrary.'

'I do?' she asked cautiously.

His eyes flickered. 'Yes. Lionel Marshall,' he said curtly. 'Owner of Orbit Publishing. They used to have Mary on their books.'

She groaned. For the first time in her life, she'd failed. Vigadó would make sure she never came anywhere near Mary. And the book was so good! She'd love to be associated with its publication.

'Till you poached her,' she said bitterly.

'Is that what he told you?' Vigadó snapped.

'Isn't it true?' Her eyes challenged his but her mouth was tremulous. Against all her common sense, she wanted Lionel to be lying.

'Hang around. You might find out,' he drawled.

'I won't sleep with you again!' she grated.

He gave a lascivious grin. 'Sleep? I wouldn't give you the chance to sleep!'

'You know what I mean. You've had your ration of sex!' she said coldly. 'I've cured you of your impotence—though I wish to God I hadn't!'

'You don't mean that, Mariann,' he murmured softly, his gaze stripping her where she stood. 'If we hadn't met, we would never have known what lovemaking could be like when two minds, bodies and emotions are in complete harmony.' Shaken by the fervour in his tone, she grabbed at the desk for support as her legs buckled under her. His dark, wickedly sensual eyes rested avidly on her. 'I will never sit at that desk again without thinking of you, the light gleaming on your skin, when you sprawled naked——'

'Please!' she begged angrily. 'You *swine*!'

'Oh, I'll beat you with the truth till it sinks into your dense head!' he muttered tightly. 'Perhaps...yes, I think you should meet Mary——'

'What trick are you playing now? It's Saturday afternoon!' she cried irritably. 'She'll have been waiting hours to meet us. If she's got any sense, she'll have gone off somewhere on her own.'

'I had the foresight to cancel today's meeting and re-arrange it for Tuesday,' he said blandly. 'Knowing what we'd be doing instead.'

'You—you *knew*?' she spluttered, bristling.

He shrugged. 'I was right, wasn't I?' he said, with inescapable truth. 'Mariann, you're standing between two warring men, each of whom is prepared to vilify the other. I'm not ashamed of anything I've done——'

'You wouldn't be, would you?' she said hotly. 'You don't have any morals or ethics——'

'Meet Mary,' he snapped. 'I will give you the opportunity to coax her back to Lionel Marshall.'

'You're pretty sure of yourself!' she said haughtily.

'Yes, I am,' he growled.

'I said before,' she said defiantly, 'you think you can hold people by fear or money alone, but in the end they will go where their hearts and souls dictate.'

'And I can win hearts and souls,' he said in clipped tones. 'Can't I?'

'I don't know what you mean,' she said huskily.

'I think you do.' He grinned disarmingly and laced his shoes. 'You unwisely taunted me about hearts and souls. You were so smug, so sure of yourself—sublimely confident that I was such an insensitive lecher that my only skill was in arousing women's sexual desires. Red rag to a bull, Mariann,' he murmured. 'My pride was wounded. I calculated that if I pulled enough heart-strings you might soften up, even half fall in love with me.'

She froze. It had been a set-up. And she'd obliged him nicely! 'That sob-story about losing your daughter——!' she began angrily.

'Is no sob-story!' he said indignantly. 'I confided in you because I wanted you to know everything about me. Nearly everything,' he amended.

'And your impotence?' she asked harshly.

'Oh, yes,' he growled. 'That was true.'

Fortunately he wasn't looking at her, or he would have seen the glittering rage that transformed her face. She'd been duped, right from the start! Vigadó had decided to play with her, a deadly game that involved capturing her emotions. He'd even pretended to be falling in love with her! She clenched her fists. In a calculating bid for her sympathies, he'd unfairly traded on the tragedies in his life and melted her heart!

The man had concrete under his skin! Arrogant, conceited, malicious, conniving...! Ready to burst with fury, she turned away, strolling as casually as she could to the window, knowing that control was all-important. Gazing out over the frozen city, she felt her heart ice over too. Vigadó was ruthless. So was she.

Fire flowed through her veins. She'd coax Mary back. She'd show him that he couldn't win in the end. He might get what he wanted temporarily, but permanent loyalty, love and affection demanded something more than clever trickery. She'd beat him yet!

CHAPTER NINE

'You took a risk, telling me,' Mariann observed flatly.

'I take risks in my business every day of my life,' he said. 'Mostly they're calculated risks, based on the facts I know,' he added smoothly.

Mariann sensed the tension in his voice. He wanted her to agree. He needed her! She was a sop to his sexual ego. The woman who'd made him a man. And she regretted that with every ounce of her being.

Smug. Assured. Self-satisfied... The pleasure of taking the opportunity he was giving her and turning it to her advantage was too tempting—and somehow she had to gain back her own self-respect. 'I can't deny that you've stolen part of my heart,' she said huskily. 'But I don't like it.'

He smiled. 'The situation is something of a mixed blessing for me too,' he said wryly. 'Granted, we could have the kind of relationship other people only read about, but I've just let Lindi go from my life in an attempt to save my sanity. I wasn't looking for anything or anyone to fill the gap, I assure you—I've neglected my business too much as it is. I suggest we give each other a little space.'

'The decorating?' she said uncertainly.

'I think András and János can survive without you. You're not welcome in the office—unless it's for sex with me, after hours,' he drawled. 'You can come and entertain me any time you want. But I suggest you take a break. We'll meet up on Tuesday. You want to meet Mary, don't you?'

Mastering the impulse to run at him and score ten more scars into his smug face, she inhaled deeply and nodded curtly. 'All right.' Two days, three nights without him. The prospect was dismal.

'Wondering what to do with yourself?' he asked softly.

'I'll do some sightseeing. I've always wanted to learn more about my mother's heritage,' she said in a forlorn voice. It would have been more enjoyable with Vigadó. Her mouth drooped. He possessed her. Darn it, she was obsessed by him!

He came over and gently held her shoulders. 'I don't want to leave you,' he said huskily, and groaned when she turned tear-filled eyes to his. 'But I think I should. You need a rest and some cooling-off time. I have to think, to work.'

'Authors to poach, editors to head-hunt,' she said resentfully.

'Of course.' He grinned. 'Enjoy the next couple of days.' His warm mouth briefly closed over hers and she shuddered as a storm of emotion battered her confused mind. 'I'll walk you back to the Hilton.'

'Thanks.' Her listless body stiffened at the steely glitter in his dark eyes. 'What is it?' she moaned, knowing she couldn't take anything more.

'You didn't correct me when I said I'd take you back to the Hilton,' he said softly.

Wearily she closed her eyes, swaying on her feet. When would he ever stop trying to trick her? 'How long have you known I'm staying there?' she asked with a sigh.

'Since I left you at the taxi rank,' he said curtly. 'I bribed the driver to return and tell me where he took you. Apparently you tipped him heavily and walked off into the night. He followed you to the Hilton and saw you collect your room key.'

'You suspected me for some time!' she breathed.

He nodded. 'It did occur to me that poverty-stricken decorators wouldn't usually stay in the best suite of a luxury hotel,' he said sarcastically. 'And everything you did made me more suspicious. Till I finally unravelled the whole truth.'

Not all, she thought, rallying a little. By the time he did, she'd be back in England, hopefully with Mary in tow. No, *definitely*. If it meant telling Mary what he'd done to her, she'd expose him for the evil brute he was. No man played with her emotions. No man would ever dominate her.

'Lionel said you were relentless,' she said, managing a rueful smile. 'I never had a chance, did I?'

'None. So rest and relax.' His hand closed around her neck lightly. 'But I will let you go only if you promise you'll help me do the tour with our esteemed author, and that you'll remain impartial and pleasant till I have gained Mary's confidence sufficiently for us all to sit down and discuss what happened between her and Lionel.'

'Ye-e-s,' she said grudgingly. 'I promise.' Mary would be wary of *her*, too. It might take a while before they could talk freely. So he didn't know Mary. She supposed Mary had been too busy finishing the book to take time out. And she had never met the shy, reclusive Irishwoman either. 'You've had nothing to do with her up to now, then?' she said.

'No.' His fingers stroked her throat speculatively. 'I didn't want to rock the boat. She's always had a strong attachment to my senior editor, Liz, who's been our contact with Mary, making all the arrangements while I've directed from the sidelines.'

Mariann's head snapped up. 'I'm aware that Liz is Lionel's wife,' she said accusingly. A stab of jealousy made her clutch at her heart.

'You are tired,' soothed Vigadó, his eyes glowing. 'We both need a shower and a sleep after that wild orgy.'

She bridled at his description but was too tired to argue and demurely nodded and let him escort her back. Externally she might look calm and resigned to following everything he suggested. Internally there was a seething cauldron of emotions and wild impulses seeking release. Wearily she leaned against him as they walked back and she wondered melodramatically if she'd ever feel bubbly again.

Mariann's sister noticed her unusual glumness immediately, when she rang that evening. After some teasing and coaxing she told Sue everything. Almost everything. There were some details she preferred not to think about, let alone reveal. As usual, Sue was common sense itself, a practical, down-to-earth confidante.

'I've never felt like this before,' she said shakily. 'I don't like it!'

'Poor Mariann,' sympathised Sue. 'You hate anyone threatening your stability, don't you? He sounds wonderful, you idiot! Grab him!'

'He *is* wonderful—and he isn't!' she wailed. 'I think I get glimpses of someone who has the potential to be warm and caring, incredibly tender and protective—and then he shatters my illusions with brutal reality. He's deceitful and ruthless and uses anything and anyone for his own ends. I don't trust him further than I could throw Arnold Schwarzenegger and I can't *bear* the "putty in his hands" bit!'

'So you want a guy who's predictable, malleable and obedient?' scathed Sue. 'Someone you don't much care for? A guy whose movements are as regular as clockwork? Sex every Saturday, golf on Sunday, bridge on Tuesday——'

'Oh, shut up!' Mariann snapped. 'I hate you when you're so *right*!' Sue laughed till Mariann ruefully chuckled too. 'Hon,' she said in despair, 'I'm horrified that I ache for such an unworthy man, terrified of the feelings I've unleashed. They swallow me up. I'm ashamed of enjoying the sex so much that I want it again and again...' Her voice became too husky to speak the words coherently.

'You want him now?' asked Sue with loving warmth.

'Mmm.' Only with Sue could she have admitted that— or let her voice sound like a whimper. Mariann sighed.

'Do you think he loves you?'

'Of course he doesn't!' she cried in astonishment.

'I'd bet a pound to his billion that he does,' said Sue.

'He never said so!'

'He's a man, isn't he?' Sue scathed.

'But he *deliberately* set out to make me fall for him!' raged Mariann.

'That doesn't mean he only wanted you for sex,' said her sister calmly. 'Only that he wanted you. Also it seems he's a good judge of character if he realised you could only be won over if your heart was touched. Most men up to now have thought you jump into bed whenever asked. He chose to seduce your soft heart. Unlike any other guy you've known, he saw that you were sensitive and tender-hearted beneath that fizzy, throw-away glamour and loin-watering allure. You must admit——' she giggled '—you've made a lot of loins water, Mariann. And you've always despised the men who never noticed anything else about you. It's not surprising you hold a grudging respect for this one.'

'Why did I ring you?' Mariann muttered irritably.

'Because I tell you the truth and we know each other better than anyone on earth,' laughed Sue. 'Though I think that might change with Vigadó about. He sounds clever and wise and gorgeous. Bring him home. I'll give him the once-over.'

Mariann giggled. 'I do love you!' she said affectionately. 'But I've got to sort out this business with Lionel. I still can't get him—or his office.'

'I think he's a deeply suspicious character,' observed Sue.

'You didn't see his distress when his wife left,' defended Mariann.

'And why did his wife leave?'

'Because...' She paused as something occurred to her. She hadn't told Sue about Vigadó's impotency. But if he was telling the truth—if—then he wouldn't have taken Liz as his mistress and Lionel had been misleading her. 'I don't know.' She sighed.

'Find out. It's the key,' said her sister wisely.

When Mariann finished the call, she lay awake for some time, trying to be as objective as Sue. It was impossible, of course. Whether she liked it or not, she was infatuated with Vigadó. He had definitely become her obsession. Despite her careful plans to avoid excessive behaviour, she'd finally followed the rest of her family in feeling passionately about something—someone—to the exclusion of everything else.

'Desperate of Devon,' she said ruefully, playing her own agony aunt, 'shape up—or surrender!'

Wearing a long, coral crushed-velvet dress that clung all the way down to her knees and then flared out to her ankle boots, she walked into Gerbeaud's, the smart coffee house that fronted the whole of the central square. Several businessmen and ladies of a certain age paused in their endearing passion for gossip, discussing life,

emotions and politics, and stared at her as she strode
through the tables. Her body-skimming dress had been
unbuttoned to the thigh and flowed open to reveal her
long, slender legs encased in black tights. She smiled on
them all, searching for Vigadó.

'Mariann! Over here!'

Her heart leapt to hear his voice. She felt the familiar
dreaminess coming over her again—and fought it.

He'd chosen a table by the window to watch the world
go by. Close beside him sat a dark-haired woman in her
thirties—overdressed, over made-up and over him.
Mariann felt indignation welling up inside her as she
walked on through the airy, high-ceilinged room, all
stucco and chandeliers and waitresses in covetable soft
white boots, laced from the open toe to the top.

'Vigadó! *Dahling*!' She smiled warmly and responded
with more enthusiasm than she meant to when he kissed
her affectionately on each cheek. If her body language
was telling Mrs All-Over anything, she thought grimly,
it ought to proclaim that Vigadó wasn't available. 'Love
your suit,' she said huskily, touching the fine grey fabric.

'Love your jacket,' he murmured, his eyes twinkling
with sardonic amusement as he stroked the hot-pink
velvet, with its high, stand-up collar. 'Eye-wincing
colours as usual. And the hat is stunning.'

'Isn't it just?' Laughing, she flipped off the floppy-
brimmed cerise hat and placed it on a spare chair, her
eyes slanting to Vigadó's companion. Not Mary—she'd
seen the covers of enough of her books to know that.
Too flashy for an editor. Then who? Her stomach
churned. A mistress-in-waiting? Or... mistress fulfilled? She winced. Now she'd unleashed his sexuality,
he'd probably gone berserk, she thought miserably. 'In-
troduce me.' She smiled tightly.

'This is our British author,' he began.

Mariann blinked. 'But you said we were...! She's not
Mary O'Brien! I know what Mary looks like!' she cried
angrily, instantly suspecting another trick.

'I certainly am not Mary O'Brien,' said the woman
icily. 'Vanessa Brewer.' She extended an unenthusi-
astic hand.

'How do you do?' Mariann said automatically.
'Vigadó——'

'Have some coffee,' he said silkily. 'And a pastry.'
She took two. 'Isn't Mary——?'

'I think you're a little muddled, darling,' he murmured suavely. 'I said I'd arranged for a British author
to come over. I can't recall saying it would be Mary.'

'You said you'd cancelled Saturday's meeting and
rearranged it for Tuesday!' she accused.

'I did. Vanessa was very understanding.' He turned
from the astounded Mariann to the dark-haired woman.
'Mariann's got her dates mixed up. We're seeing Mary
later. I'm certain I didn't say it was *Mary* today.' He
grinned. 'In fact, I was careful not to. Remember,
darling? We arranged on Saturday to show Vanessa
around Budapest today, Tuesday,' he said softly. And,
whispering in her ear, he muttered, 'You promised faith-
fully to help me do the tour with this woman and to
remain impartial and pleasant.'

'So I did,' she said, hiding her fury. He'd deliberately
enticed her by dangling the prospect of talking to a
British author. He'd *known* she would expect Mary! The
man was a sadist. 'In England we call that kind of
trickery being economical with the truth.'

'In Hungary, we call it inspired,' he drawled.

More days together. Wonderful. Terrible. Oh, God,
he was stretching her on a rack! But she wouldn't let
him have the satisfaction of knowing how stupid she felt.

Summing up the beringed woman quickly, she said
brightly, 'Well, Vanessa, I'm looking forward to all the
fascinating museums we're going to visit today!' She was
rewarded by a scowl from Vanessa and a grin of admiration from Vigadó.

As Vanessa began to chatter to him, pointedly excluding Mariann, it was obvious that the woman was
smitten. Another bad point about her. The fuming
Mariann wanted to kick Vigadó hard under the table,
but his legs had captured hers and were holding them
firmly. He was the most underhand, dirty, double-dealing
male she'd ever met!

She made vaguely interested noises about Vanessa's
novel, which sounded bleakly devoted to sex and

shopping and unpleasantly deviant behaviour. It seemed that the woman was trying to sound sexy by talking about certain passages in the book and hoping they'd arouse Vigadó. Mariann stiffened when Vanessa's hand touched the scar on Vigadó's face. She was glad that he didn't look too pleased, either.

'I bet there's a story behind *that*,' said Vanessa, too insensitive to notice Vigadó's involuntary flinch.

'Several,' he said drily. 'All of them lurid.'

'I wish I'd met you before I started the book,' cooed Vanessa huskily. 'You look as though you've *lived*.'

'He *has*!' enthused Mariann, wickedly recalling Sue's words. 'He's such *fun*. Golf on Sunday, bridge *every* Tuesday, and——' She coyly lowered her eyes and shifted her glass of iced water about the green marble table. 'You're broad-minded, I know,' she simpered, lifting her gaze to Vanessa's. 'So I can tell you. Sex *every* Saturday at ten o'clock, without fail!'

'You have icing sugar all around your mouth,' murmured Vigadó, coming at her with his napkin. She lifted her face and pouted provocatively. 'Thanks for increasing my dullness factor,' he whispered, his amused eyes glued to hers. 'And for making this more enjoyable than I expected.'

'I want to go shopping and get my hair done,' announced Vanessa sulkily, apparently loathing not to be the centre of attention.

'Of course, anything you wish—though your hair looks lovely as it is,' smiled Vigadó gallantly. Mariann wrinkled her nose, thinking how easily he lied. Vanessa's hair looked as if it had been lacquered to death. 'I think you'd like our pedestrianised Váci utca and its boutiques. It leads off the square.'

He rose, kissed Vanessa's hand, helped her into her coat and then offered her his arm. Mariann trudged along behind them, hating the way she felt about Vanessa and how bitchy her thoughts were, but incensed to see him flirting and being gentlemanly with the vain, affected woman. Vanessa was having difficulty with her high heels on the cobbles but Vigadó was patiently guiding her in a surprisingly considerate way.

'She must have known she'd be sightseeing!' muttered Mariann irritably while Vanessa dived into yet another boutique. 'Why are you so nice to her when she's too vain to wear sensible shoes?'

'She's a silly woman but that's no reason for me to let her break her ankle, is it?' He tipped back the brim of Mariann's hat and bent to kiss her beneath it.

'You're right,' she said, shamefaced. 'I'm mean.'

'A little green round the gills, perhaps,' he grinned. 'I'm glad you're with me. She's terminally boring.'

'Serves you right,' said Mariann heartlessly. 'You tricked me into thinking I'd be meeting Mary. I won't promise you anything ever again. Or trust you.'

'I think you will,' he said confidently, kissing her tenderly.

'Don't do that!' she snapped.

'You love it,' he said and did it again.

She loved it. Hated *him*.

'Vigadó!' Vanessa's grating voice interrupted their embrace and they jumped apart guiltily. 'I'm going to be some time,' the woman said. 'They have a beauty salon here. A couple of hours at least, they said. After that, I'd like to meet you for dinner. Alone,' she said pointedly. 'We have a lot I want to talk about.'

'Of course,' he agreed. 'Some of those sex scenes need a little attention.' Vanessa beamed triumphantly and licked her lips at the thought of them both reading through some steamy pages, but Mariann thought he meant they needed editing. She hoped she was right. 'Will you be able to find your way back to the hotel?' he enquired solicitously.

Mariann fumed. The woman wasn't incapable! She'd managed to fly all the way from London on her own! And then she grinned at her indignation, recognising it for what it was—jealousy.

'I'll go, then. Bye!' she called brightly to them both. They were engrossed in making arrangements to meet later. 'Have a lovely dinner.'

But she didn't mean it, she thought gloomily. Ridiculous it might be, sour grapes too, but she wanted them to be served underdone lobster, *gulyás* that stripped the roof off their mouths and left their lips numb, and creamy puddings that made them sick! Oh, heaven help her, she'd got it bad!

She paused to let two mounted policemen by, the horses' hooves slipping and sliding on the cobbles. A familiar hand grasped her arm protectively and she groaned.

'Have you seen the crown? King Stephen's crown?' murmured Vigadó in her ear. 'I'd like to——'

'No!' she snapped, annoyed that he'd followed, and turned blindly to look in a shop window.

'This is a good toy shop, if you're interested,' he said in amusement.

'I am, as a matter of fact,' she replied haughtily. Her eyes had caught sight of a doll in traditional costume. 'I'd like to get one of those for my sister Sue.'

'The one on the phone who raved about some Mexican shirt she'd made from her flat-mate's sheets?' he chuckled.

'Yes,' she replied, her face soft with affection. 'That's Sue! She'd love the embroidery on this doll's dress and the layered petticoats.'

'How old is she?' he said curiously.

'Twenty-one, and no, before you ask; I'm not buying her a doll because she's mentally disadvantaged! She's crazy about design, particularly folk costume.' Her face glowed. 'I adore her,' she admitted. 'I adore all my family.'

'You're very lucky,' he said quietly. 'I envy you. What does your sister do? Does she have a job?'

'Mmm. She began working for a London fashion house, but now she's making costumes for Glyndebourne, the small opera house in Sussex. I don't think it's what she wants to do, but she knows the experience will stand her in good stead when she starts her own business.'

'She's as ambitious as you.'

Mariann smiled. 'Yes. She's a terrible workaholic. Do you think the doll will be expensive?'

'Only one way to find out,' he said, opening the door for her.

'Vigadó! *Szervusz, szervusz!*'

Mariann watched in amusement as Vigadó was soundly kissed by a group of women in the shop who evidently knew him very well. She supposed he'd bought a lot of toys for his daughter. While he was exchanging news with the assistants, she wandered around, enchanted. It must be the least stuffy doll shop she'd ever seen, the staff in knee-length black shorts and purple T-shirts with the English words 'Excellent Service' embroidered on them in gold. The shelves were stacked from floor to ceiling with stuffed and wooden toys, weird, ingenious and wonderful.

'So this is where you spend your leisure hours!' she teased, opening an egg. A little bird inside it began to cheep and she beamed. 'Isn't it cute?'

'Yes . . . Unfortunately, it would break in transit. This would be all right,' he mused, somewhat mystifyingly.

He was examining a fluffy white monkey and one of the assistants seemed to be reeling off its merits. Mariann thought he was casting rather a critical eye over the toys and when he soberly assessed the squeezability of a ridiculous purple and yellow spotted dinosaur her curiosity was really aroused.

'I'll take fifty of each,' he said in Hungarian, then something else she didn't understand.

'Fifty spotty dinosaurs?' She grinned. 'How about this one? It's got a squelchy tummy and a rustling tail. That would keep you amused during dinner with Vanessa tonight!'

'*Ötven,*' he said to the assistant, ordering fifty of those too. He smiled to Mariann's astonishment. 'I order consignments of toys for refugee children,' he explained. Before she could even express her amazement, he'd moved to examine the realistic-looking dolls.

She didn't want to believe him. István was involved with refugees, and she'd been very impressed when she'd heard of his dedication. 'Refugees?' she repeated casually.

'That's why I was interested when you mentioned the Kastély Huszár,' he said, browsing along the shelves. 'I don't know the countess but I met her son István a couple of times on border runs. We each drove lorries into Romania last year, to supply children's homes.'

Her heart somersaulted with a sudden pang of emotion and she knew at once that he wasn't lying. István kept his refugee work very private. 'I'm amazed,' she said faintly. 'You personally provide toys for refugee children and drive lorry-loads——'

'It's not a big deal. What else would I do with my money? I learnt long ago that when you have it you don't need it so badly. I have one beautiful house and a flat, one car, sufficient cash to pay twenty per cent of my income to Eva and Lindi and some left over for myself, as a reward for my hard work. The rest is superfluous. I take over toys, medical supplies, beds, general supplies,' he said in a matter-of-fact tone.

'But you give your time and effort,' she said soberly. 'For a businessman, that's worth a lot more than the money. Most people wouldn't bother.'

'István does——' he began.

'He was a refugee,' she said quietly. 'And you?'

'We're all refugees in one way or another,' he said huskily and turned to chat amiably to the dark-haired manageress.

Her heart thudded. She was running from her emotions. Was he? Whatever the reason for it, his generosity and compassion disturbed her. Mariann tried to make that fit in with the heartless tyrant she'd psyched herself up to despise and found suddenly that her anger against him was melting away and was being replaced by admiration.

Needing a while to consider this, she took her time choosing a doll for Sue, also partly because there were so many ethnic costumes and partly because she was fascinated by the way Vigadó was being treated by the staff in the shop. He seemed relaxed and at ease, occasionally serious and concerned, sometimes teasing a young assistant about her new hairstyle, sometimes discussing the virtues of a toy that was brought for him to admire.

But the most interesting thing for Mariann was that the staff here all liked and respected him. In their eyes and their gestures she saw the same devotion that had gradually coloured the looks and body language of everyone in his office. Common sense told her that he couldn't fool all of those people, all of the time. Charisma won people over; it didn't hold them.

She pretended to be deciding between two dolls, her mind whirling. If he was liked by people he worked with, if he gave not only his money but also his time and labour in easing the hardships of refugee children and those in Romanian institutions, then . . . then he wasn't the devil that Lionel had painted.

She tried to think of one thing Lionel had done for others. Of one person in the office who hadn't grumbled about him, even in the short time she'd been there. Her face grew pale. Now who was the baddy?

Her teeth dug into her lower lip. She didn't know whether she wanted to meet Mary now. The last thing she wanted was to discover that Mary had a good reason for ditching Lionel as her editor and publisher. She needed Vigadó to be in the wrong.

Otherwise . . . Mariann gripped the doll tightly. Otherwise there would be nothing in the way of her love for him. The thought made her tremble with fear and apprehension.

A subdued Mariann stepped out of the shop, clutching a carrier bag containing Sue's doll. Immediately, her hand was caught by Vigadó's.

'Now,' he said quietly, 'the crown.'

'Why are you so all-fired keen to show me this?' she complained, finding herself being propelled rapidly down the street.

'Because the crown is Hungary,' he said simply. Despite her reluctance, she was touched by his fervour. It stirred her that he could feel so deeply about his country. 'And it's part of your heritage, I gather,' he mused. 'How come?'

'My mother escaped over the Hungarian border when she was a young woman. She came to England as a displaced person and Father employed her,' she explained, not telling him the whole, improbable story.

'That sounds honourable, not obsessive behaviour,' he said quietly, turning his dark eyes on her, and she saw herself, obsessed, mirrored in them.

'Ours was a small community,' she said, deciding not to mention that her father had been a vicar at the time.

'Father was the victim of gossip when he took Mother into his house because everyone thought she was what they called "a fallen woman". But he felt so passionately about her that he jeopardised his job and his future, nevertheless.'

'She must have been quite a woman. And the rest of you?'

'Mother was... deeply occupied with something that rather excluded us all, so it fell to Tanya, my eldest sister, to mother us. And she almost forgot her own needs because she was so darn determined to protect and shelter us from the ravages of life!' Her eyes became limpid with love. 'Brother John has struggled since puberty to impress his childhood sweetheart, and you've heard a little about my sister Sue. She's a single-minded, talented designer with nothing but embroidery threads and the dream of a worldwide team of out-workers in her head.'

'And you?' He took her hand, kissed it and laid it on his heart. 'You?' he repeated softly.

'I don't want to feel passionately about anything or anyone,' she said huskily. 'Emotions possess you like a madness. Mother's incredible sense of duty made us all what we are—a little out of kilter, over-intense and passionate in our reactions.' She heaved a deep sigh.

'And what was she so determined to do?'

'I can't tell you,' she said gently. 'Only that she had to keep a secret for nearly the whole of her marriage—and till after her death. It embittered and alienated us and almost ruined the whole family.'

'That suggests a formidable strength and will-power,' he said thoughtfully. 'Which you've inherited. I admire single-mindedness. But not blindness.' He smiled faintly. 'Do you think you'll ever find a partner? Will you ever marry?'

'Unlikely. I'm looking for perfection,' she said with a perfunctory smile that died on her lips. He had the strength she needed in a lover, and the sensuality. But his ethics left much to be desired.

'Perfection doesn't exist,' he said quietly. 'Only in dreams. Or in that foggy, mindless state we call "love". Perhaps the trick is to give in to love and let it drag us

kicking and screaming to what we fondly think is our
perfect partner.'

'I've had enough of tricks,' she said tartly.

'So have I. And I suggest you open your eyes and
prepare yourself for the unvarnished truth. I'm determined you will, even if I have to stick myself under a
spotlight to do so.'

Staying her muttered protests, he kissed her lightly on
the cheek, escorting her up the steps of the museum
housing the coronation regalia. And when they stood in
front of the case where the Byzantine crown lay, she knew
why he'd been so eager for her to see it. The crown's
unique dome shape was encircled by a deep gold band
decorated with huge rubies, sapphires, emeralds and
pearls. Hanging on either side were slender gold chains
and crowning the top was a crooked cross. Even to her,
it had a special magic.

'How was that damaged?' she asked curiously.

Vigadó squeezed her hand. 'It's been pushed into sacks
and thrown into countless chests and spirited to safety
during its nine hundred or so years,' he said with husky
pride. 'At the first hint of invasion, the Magyar have
always protected it. You can understand why it sym-
bolises our national identity.'

'I do,' she said, sensing the almost reverential awe of
everyone in the room.

He gave her a heart-stopping smile. 'I knew you
would,' he murmured in a caressing tone. 'Hungary will
be great again, I know it. I will work night and day for
that.'

'You have quite a romantic heart for a man with a
tough hide,' she said, her heart thudding rapidly. And
she moved on to view the rest of the regalia, aware that
his passion was affecting her emotions profoundly. 'Oh,
how lovely!' she exclaimed, grateful for the diversion of
a silk robe. She strained forward to admire the angels
and prophets and apostles, embroidered in silver, the
birds and trees and flowers... 'It's dazzling,' she
breathed.

'I'm so glad you appreciate it all,' he said softly. 'It
means a great deal to me. I would do anything for my
country.' He smiled. 'I'm heartily relieved that Vanessa

isn't with us. I wanted to be alone with you when you saw this.'

'Why?' she asked warily.

'Oh,' he dissembled, 'you're half-Hungarian; the symbols of Hungary's tenacity in the face of all opposition were bound to touch your heart, weren't they?'

She frowned, the enchantment spoiled by the blatant hint of his own relentless determination to weaken her, one way or another, and they finished the tour in silence. But her heart had been touched and despite her disillusionment she let her hand stay in his.

How many men had held hands with her? None! Men had caressed her bottom—till slapped—they'd stroked her arm or her shoulder and reached for more intimate parts of her body, but they'd never offered her anything so simple, tender or as pleasurable as the sensation of walking along, holding hands with... She scowled down at her bright red boots, moving close to Vigadó's glove-soft leather shoes. In step. With the man she loved.

Once outside the museum, Vigadó looked back down the traffic-filled street expectantly. A sleek Alfa-Romeo slid half on to the pavement and Mariann slanted a suspicious look at Vigadó.

'This looks rather planned to me,' she muttered.

'I got a waiter to ring from Gerbeaud's. I'm taking you to Visegrád,' he said quietly.

CHAPTER TEN

MARIANN stared. 'Visegrád! What about Vanessa? You're supposed to be having dinner with her,' she said in surprise, torn between going and haughtily strolling away, mistress of her own destiny.

'I'll get back in time. If not, one of my staff will have to deputise. Judit would do that very well.'

Mariann eyed the liveried chauffeur doubtfully as he jumped out, greeted Vigadó with cheerful respect and held open the rear door for them. 'We *are* going to see Mary?' she queried, making sure this time.

'Yes. Hurry up, traffic's piling up,' he said testily.

She stood her ground, ignoring the baleful horns and impatient yells. 'And you'll let me talk to her and ask her any questions I want?'

'Yes. Get in,' he said shortly.

Still unsure, she did so, wishing he hadn't slid so close to her in the back seat. Their thighs were touching. She made to move away, but he merely pulled her to him and kissed her for a long, long time, caressing her soothingly till she found herself responding.

It didn't matter, she told herself. Her revenge would be sweeter when she walked away from him. That would be a real blow to his over-inflated ego. But, instead of feeling satisfied with her cleverness, she wanted to groan aloud at the thought of leaving him.

'Please, Vigadó!' she begged, pushing against his broad shoulders.

'Be merciful. I've been wanting to do that for hours,' he said huskily, his hand softly moving over her engorged breast.

'Don't!' she mumbled. 'Your driver——'

Vigadó sat back, apologising—actually apologising! Mariann was astonished. They were out of Budapest

174

now, driving through fields silent with deep snow, smoke rising from the long-houses into a sunny blue sky.

'I feel odd, being driven by a chauffeur,' she confessed nervously.

'I've never got used to it,' he admitted with a smile. 'Normally I prefer to do everything myself. But it does release me so I can work. And on this occasion it allows me to kiss you without risking instant death under a lorry!' He grinned wickedly. 'I spent all the time at Gerbeaud's struggling with a cruelly unfulfilled urge to take you in my arms and lick the pastry crumbs from your lips.'

Mariann's tongue sneaked out and moistened her dry mouth. His desire was flattering—and exciting. Desperately she tried to control her own urge to fling herself at him and lose herself in his passion.

'Vanessa would have used that for her book,' she said lightly.

'Vanessa would have walked out,' he said with a grimace.

'She fancies you.' There was disapproval in her tone. And would he notice the jealousy? she wondered anxiously.

'I know. She's always on the look-out for men to star in her next novel. Dieter landed me with her. I'm beginning to realise why,' he said ruefully. 'She wouldn't look at me if I weren't rich.'

'I think she might,' said Mariann sourly. 'You've made a very smooth transition from being poor to being rich.' Inexplicably she wanted to know everything about him, to explore his background and to know what he was like as a child, a young man, what he did in his leisure time... She gave an inward groan, recognising those signs. Tanya had told her that she'd found herself fascinated by every minute detail of István's life.

'Not as smooth as you think. My regret is that my parents never benefited,' Vigadó said quietly. Seeing her undisguised interest, he smiled faintly and settled her in the crook of his arm. 'Mother died of pneumonia during a particularly bad winter,' he continued. 'I can hardly remember her. Father...' He frowned, lines of strain

tightening his mouth. 'Father was already showing the
first signs of multiple sclerosis.'

'That explains it!' she exclaimed, remembering. 'You
said you were used to your father falling——'

'That came later.' He sighed. 'The attacks were ir-
regular at first and made him very bad-tempered. It was
a long while before I understood his difficulties. I thought
he was secretly drinking. So did everyone else. He didn't
get much sympathy. Youth is sublimely ignorant of
physical disability,' Vigadó said wryly. He touched his
scar.

Plucking up courage, she asked hesitantly, 'Tell me
the truth about that. I heard it was some fight over a
woman.'

His dark eyes met hers. 'In a way.'

Her body sank with disappointment. 'Oh,' she said
in a small voice. The rumours were true. Stiff and miserable, she stared out at the bleak winter landscape.

Vigadó picked up her hand and toyed with it for a
few moments as though making up his mind to explain.
'It's something I find difficult to speak about,' he muttered. 'But I can see you're upset so I'll tell you.'

'Please don't reveal anything you don't want to,' she
said coldly.

'Unless I do,' he replied grimly, 'you'll never understand the first thing about me.'

'I don't want to know about your women!' she
snapped.

His breath exhaled in an angry rush. 'You'll listen
when I'm talking!' he growled. 'I'm making the effort;
so can you!'

She shrugged. 'I can't stop you,' she said ungraciously.

'God give me strength! Have you ever seen a whore—
a real common-or-garden whore, not a call-girl—close
up, Mariann?'

'Not as many as you, I imagine,' she said acidly.

With difficulty, he checked his temper. 'I met one for
the first time on the day I was wondering whether to
marry Eva and leap-frog to riches. I'd just had the offer
from Dieter, had just been dropped by his chauffeur after
tea at Gundel's.' His eyes narrowed. 'I went from one
world to another in a matter of moments. I got chatting

to a Polish woman outside a coffee-house. She asked me to guess her age and I said I thought she could be close to forty. It turned out she was twenty-four. I can remember the shock I felt, even now.'

'I don't understand,' frowned Mariann.

He stared out at the snowy scenery, seeing nothing. 'She looked even older,' he said huskily. 'I thought I was flattering her by suggesting she was forty. She told me she was a prostitute, that she longed to go back to her village, and it occurred to me in a blinding flash of compassion that if I were rich I could do a lot, not only for myself, but for others, like this woman. I was an idealistic eighteen-year-old,' he muttered.

He had romance in his soul, Mariann mused. And he must have been a very impressionable young man. That made her feel tender towards him. 'Nothing wrong with ideals,' she said softly. 'That's why you married Eva?'

He shrugged. 'She loved me, I was fond of her and was responsible for her pregnancy. I thought, in my ignorance, that I could make her happy. Anyway, I borrowed money from Eva and went to find the Polish girl.'

Mariann smiled. 'That's nice.'

'No happy ending,' he muttered roughly. 'I couldn't find her anywhere. She'd completely disappeared. Her pimp heard me asking after her and I found myself in a dark alley being beaten up.'

'Were you badly hurt?' she asked anxiously.

'Bruises. A couple of broken ribs,' he said dismissively. 'That was nothing to my disappointment. I felt I'd lost the chance to help her and the thought of that woman, far from her homeland, becoming progressively degraded, filled me with one hell of a helpless frustration. And a lot of guilt and anger.'

'Which you took out on Eva,' she said in a low tone, tense within the circle of his arm.

His hand cradled her face and turned it so that she was looking into his blazing black eyes. 'No! I never hurt her,' he growled. 'Never harmed her or treated her roughly, whatever the rumours Lionel has been spreading about me all these years.'

Mariann flinched at his anger. 'You give the impression of being violent,' she said shakily.

'It was a tactic. I wanted to put the fear of God into you,' he grated. 'I wanted you to forget your arrangement with Lionel, perhaps to leave your profession altogether. I hate women being used by men. I hated myself—oh, *God*, how I hated myself!—for using you to end the farce of my dead marriage! Mariann, I had to do it for the sake of my daughter. I couldn't bear to see her being tortured by the tearing loyalties she had for us both, for the distress she was suffering in thinking that her own father was a brute.'

Released with a sudden abruptness, Mariann sat for a while digesting what he'd said. It appeared that Lionel was probably telling lies. But she couldn't be sure. She slanted a surreptitious glance up at Vigadó and her heart lurched with love. More than anything, she wanted him to be happy. He loved his daughter enough to walk out of her life to save her from pain. Perhaps...

'Does Eva know what you've just told me, about your father's illness and the Polish girl you wanted to help?' she asked quietly.

He gave a curt shake of his head. 'I haven't told anyone.'

Mariann was shaken by that. Flattered, honoured. Why me? she asked herself, and didn't dare to believe the answer.

'Vigadó,' she said unsteadily, 'if you tell her, confide in her, I think she might understand. It's a very touching story. She thinks—as everyone does—that you married her for her money and because she was pregnant——'

'That's about it,' he said harshly.

'You're too hard on yourself. You genuinely hoped to save the world.' She smiled. 'Impossible though that is, Eva might find that as touching...' bravely she put herself on the line '...as heart-warming and as admirable as I do,' she said huskily. 'You were only eighteen. I'm sure she'll understand and will be glad you weren't totally cold-blooded. I think you ought to come clean with Eva and why she found us together, then perhaps you can both talk about Lindi's future,' she said, lifting her earnest face to his.

'Would she?' He frowned uncertainly.

'She's a woman. We are touched by the same emotions,' she replied. 'However we may pretend we aren't. And we do find tenderness deeply appealing.'

'I think she might,' he said slowly. 'I really think she might! Mariann! You,' he said huskily, kissing her with tenderness, 'are melting my heart.'

In desperation, she tore herself away, realising he must be grateful to her for giving him hope in reclaiming his daughter. 'Then I'd better shut up,' she said with false jollity. 'You'll be needing that heart later, for Lindi.'

There was an unnatural brightness in his eyes when he looked at her before bending his head to kiss her hand. His lips lingered and the pain of love lanced through her. She'd tell him to turn the car around, that she didn't want to see Mary and be forced through a sense of loyalty to try and persuade Mary to return to Lionel; all she did know was that she wanted to live with Vigadó for as long as he needed her.

He jerked his head up and Mariann realised the car was coming to a smooth stop. 'Not long,' he said huskily. 'We cross the Danube here.'

Her moment had gone. Just as well. How would her family feel if she devoted herself to a man with no ethics? How would she feel, when he eventually dumped her? She had to remember that Vigadó was utterly ruthless as far as women were concerned, and that her fantasising about his 'good nature' was largely wishful thinking.

They were all refugees and she must run from a love that would destroy her.

Tense and wound up, she sat swamped in misery while the chauffeur bought tickets for the ferry and then drove on to it, behind two lorries transporting wine. The drivers chatted and exchanged gossip and Vigadó wandered over to them, leaving her in the car. The river slid by, flat and silvery, bending between picturesque hills and forests, and she felt very lonely and rejected, her sad eyes watching the men talking and laughing. She would have given anything to be with them, enjoying the icy air on her face and the wonderful scenery, hanging on to Vigadó's arm.

Irritated with herself, she huddled into the corner of the car and tried to get a grip on herself.

'A few more miles,' said Vigadó, scrambling in, his face glowing with cold.

She ignored him. A few more miles. And then it would all end.

'That's Visegrád.'

Her moist lashes lifted at his eagerness and she peered out. Perched on top of a great outcrop was a citadel, its reflection mirrored in the icy waters of the Danube. She shrank back, watching the road as it wound upwards, giving panoramic views of the broad river and snow-clad hills. Eventually they turned off and drove between a pair of manorial gates.

'My house,' he said softly.

Mariann's tearful eyes widened. The car was stopping in front of a breathtaking baroque palace set in ornamental gardens high above the Danube that glittered in the late afternoon sun far below.

'Your house!' she exclaimed shakily.

He smiled faintly at her astonishment and courteously guided her up the flight of stone steps. 'Mary!' he said in pleasure as a woman ran out from beneath the elaborate stone portico.

'Dear Vigadó! Welcome to your own house!' she cried enthusiastically in a broad Irish accent.

And Mariann's heart sank. Sensible Mary had been captivated by him, like all the rest. Why else was she hugging the breath out of him?

'You must be Mariann,' said Mary shyly. 'I've been talking to Vigadó about you solidly for the last few days——'

Mariann clenched her fists. 'And he told you what to say,' she muttered bitterly.

Mary laughed. 'And me a writer? No one tells me what to say! The blarney is the one thing I'm good at—that and making tea. Come on in and have a decent cup of tea, Irish style. I don't hold with all this continental coffee.'

Vigadó groaned and raised his eyes to heaven. Resisting the instant appeal of Mary's gentle character, Mariann walked stiffly into a comfortable sitting-room and perched on the edge of a chair, a bold statement in the subtle, elegant room. She snatched off her hat and flung it on to the brocade seat.

'I don't want to take too long over this,' she said tightly. 'So let's get to the point. I want to know why you left Lionel, when he'd nursed you as a writer and helped you through crises and——'

'Lionel?' interrupted Mary with an incredulous expression. 'You must be chasing fairies! Lionel's about as much use to an author as a stone tablet!'

'That's ridiculous! He started Orbit; he built it up——' blazed Mariann angrily.

'Not at all,' said Mary firmly. 'It's been Liz, all along. She's the creative one. She built the company. Lionel couldn't recognise the talent of Shakespeare himself if the Bard stood up in front of him and rattled off *Romeo and Juliet*!'

'You're lying!' cried Mariann furiously.

'Am I?' Mary's mouth firmed ominously. 'Then why do you think the bank would only back Orbit if Liz and I were still there as collateral? Lionel was a front man—good at publicity, covering for Liz because she's even shyer than I am.'

Mariann blinked. True, Liz had the reputation of always keeping to the background, but... 'Is that the story?' she asked scornfully.

'It's true as God is my witness,' Mary replied.

Mariann dropped her eyes and absently played with the buttons on the front of her skirt. It was possible. Mary wouldn't lie like that; she was known to be a strong and devout Catholic. Mariann's mind raced. She remembered the grumbling comparisons drawn by the staff of Orbit over the piles of typescripts in Liz's office and Lionel's clear desk. She'd thought he was neat and efficient, that the mutterings from the rest of the staff were sour grapes.

Her eyes searched Mary's frank blue ones and she knew it was true and that she'd been half expecting it. 'But don't you think you had a loyalty to the company?' she insisted stiffly.

'I did,' Mary agreed. 'When Liz and Lionel broke up and she finally made the break with him and Orbit, I did my best to work with him. He nearly ruined my confidence with his constant carpings and criticisms and downright stupid suggestions!'

Vigadó leaned forward. 'Mary was frantic. She couldn't write, couldn't cope with Lionel's extraordinary interference,' he said. 'The relationship between author and editor is crucial—you must know that.'

'Yes,' said Mariann slowly.

Vigadó smiled at her reluctance. 'She sent him a letter and explained that she had made such a good professional relationship with Liz that she was forced to follow her, wherever she worked. And she told him, in a very frank way, that he should never try to act as anyone's editor again because he had a unique ability to destroy talent instead of fostering it.'

'That's why I hid,' said Mary. 'He would have followed me to the ends of the earth and kept badgering me, and where would that have left me, with my book not finished and the best scenes yet to write?'

With shaking hands, Mariann picked up her cup and put it down again without taking a sip, dreading to admit to herself that everything she'd done had been a waste of time. Mary was happy. Under Liz's guidance and encouragement, she'd written a wonderful book that would be an instant bestseller.

'You didn't poach her?' she asked Vigadó in a small voice.

'No,' he answered gently. 'Lionel's authors flooded to me when Liz left. That made Lionel look a fool and he was very angry. He's tried for some time to discredit me. He's a vicious bastard——'

Her head jerked up and her eyes were pained and accusing. 'But you are just as bad!' she flung. 'Your tactics leave much to be desired! You are calculating and ruthless——'

'Not as ruthless as you've heard,' he said quietly. 'Don't get me wrong, I'm no angel. I was trained in Dieter's mould. But most of the dubious deals have been initiated and handled by Dieter himself. I am in the process of changing those tactics. We're big enough to attract business without resorting to underhand means.'

'How can I believe that?' she muttered rebelliously, wanting to, afraid to.

'The evidence of your own eyes and ears,' he suggested. 'I don't know why you're so damn determined to see Lionel's side. I know he put a job your way, but can't you see what he's been doing? He knew his company was folding. There was nothing he could do about that. He wanted to bring me down too by hiring you to find Mary, and perhaps to ruin my "marriage". Luckily I'd been warned——'

'By Liz?' she asked resentfully.

'Yes.'

'Poor Lionel!' she said hotly. 'Betrayed by his wife!'

Vigadó just looked at her. 'Can you imagine how Liz must have felt to be forced to tell me that she feared Lionel was intending to cause trouble?' he asked softly. 'She was worried because she'd let slip that I was coming to Budapest earlier than expected. She didn't want me to be hurt any more. Liz is a good woman. Gentle, kind. She's respected and admired throughout the publishing world, adored by her authors. There isn't a cruel bone in her body. What does that tell you about her opinion of Lionel if she's prepared to tell me what he may be up to?'

Mariann didn't want to answer. She needed to feel some sympathy for Lionel or she'd fling herself at Vigadó's feet, beg his forgiveness and be his slave for ever. What a prospect!

She jumped up and restlessly wandered about the room. Lionel had made sure he'd known everything she was going to do. She remembered what Lionel had said about men finding her sexy and blushed, knowing in her heart of hearts that he'd hoped that merely by being in the office she would land up in bed with the supposedly sex-mad Vigadó. A gamble, throwing a supposedly sexy woman in the path of a man with a reputation of being an international rake. But it had come off, despite the obstacles that Lionel had known nothing about.

She ran over the other evidence. The dolly-bird wig. The instructions to act like a cheerful 'floosie'. Lionel had set her up. She'd trusted the man. Put herself

through all this... Her hands clenched and she began
to shake. Suddenly she felt humiliated and dirty. Used.
'Men!' she grated.
'I think,' said Mary delicately, 'that you two ought to
talk a little and sort this out between you, so I'll leave
you to it.'
'Thanks, Mary,' Vigadó said quietly. 'Can you ring
my office and ask Judit to collect Vanessa—say I'm held
up out of town, offer my apologies and give her flowers,
a champagne dinner and gypsy music?'
'Sure. Oh, before I go, Vigadó,' Mary said, 'I took a
call for you. From an acquaintance of yours—István
something ... yes, Huszár.' Mariann stiffened, her eyes
wide. 'He said he and Tanya——' Mariann cringed, her
stomach knotted with fear '—were setting up dinner with
Tanya's sister Mariann—same name as yours——!' Mary
smiled at the white-faced figure by the window '—and
would like you to make up a foursome.' The Irishwoman
had reached the door. 'It could be interesting. He said
Mariann was in publishing.'
She left. Mariann couldn't move. There was a long
silence.
'You have a sister called Tanya,' he said hoarsely.
She couldn't speak.
'And this ... Mariann is in publishing,' he went on relentlessly. 'That wouldn't be you, by any chance, would
it?' he snarled.
She nodded.
'My God!' he seethed, rising to his feet. 'You're
working for Lionel! You're not a call-girl after all—
you're one of his editors!'
'Yes,' she whispered nervously. He'd sworn that if she
deceived him he'd tear her apart. Her breathing was
ragged, catching in her dry throat.
'You bitch!' he growled. 'You're in league with
Lionel!'
'Yes—no—I—— Don't come near me!' she yelled,
seeing the glint in his malevolent black eyes.
'A professional hooker I can understand. But you
willingly allowed yourself to be seduced by me to save
his business—or perhaps you knew it was just to help
him get his revenge on me! That makes you a calculating

little whore!' he roared, striding towards her. 'I hope you rot in hell—and I'm going to kick you there, now!'

She gave a terrified cry, turned and frantically opened the French doors on to the terrace, a bright splash of colour stumbling in the snow, plunging blindly on while Vigadó gained ground, his feet crunching unnervingly close behind her. And then he was hauling her around, shaking her roughly, his face suffused with a rage so terrible that she sobbed with fear.

'I didn't know! I didn't know it was revenge, I swear!' she wailed.

'You would say that, wouldn't you?' he snarled, pushing her against a tree. Snow fell on them from its shaken branches, making them gasp with shock. 'And I fell for you!' he roared. 'You, a woman who regards her body so cheaply——'

'I don't!' she yelled, struggling in his arms. 'I was a *virgin*!'

'The hell you were!'

'It's true! Lionel set me up! I was only going to get Mary's address, I swear, I swear! You took my virginity away from me and...' She stopped, staring at him in astonishment. 'What did you say, about falling for me?' she breathed.

'Nothing!' he said savagely.

'You did, you——'

'*No*!' he bit out, glowering at her with baleful eyes. 'As for your being a virgin, you were a pretty skilled, responsive virgin,' he scathed. 'And I'm going to do what I've been wanting to do all day, but have restrained myself because I foolishly wanted to respect you. You've made an idiot out of me,' he seethed. 'No woman does that. My God, I'm going to make you regret that! I know how to make you crawl!'

'I—— Oh!' She was suddenly on her back in the snow, Vigadó's hands tearing violently at her clothes. 'No, please! Please!' she cried in distress. 'Don't think badly of me! I never agreed to seduce you—I *was* a virgin; ask Tanya, ask István... my father's a *vicar*——'

'Bitch,' he muttered savagely.

'I swear!' she wailed. 'Do you think he didn't bring me up to honour my body? Why do you think I've been so confused and horrified by what I did?' To her relief, his fingers had stilled and he was scowling darkly at her. But he was listening. And she loved him, couldn't bear to think that he thought she'd behaved badly. So she took a gamble again. 'You made love to me and...' she blushed '...it was unbelievable. Everything we did seemed natural and...wonderful. I hadn't been touched like that, kissed like that... I'd never felt as if I wanted to die in a man's arms before.'

'Mariann? Tears?' He tentatively touched her face and she flinched.

'I love you; I can't bear to think of leaving you,' she said huskily. 'I thought I was infatuated at first, because you'd given me the most amazing sexual experience. Now I know that it's far more than that. I'm scared, Vigadó, because I know you'll probably end up hurting me, but I have to be with you.' She smiled weakly. 'My heart is in your hands. I have to be where my heart is, don't I?'

With a low groan, he pulled her into his arms. 'Love! It comes, doesn't it, even when you don't want it?' He kissed her gently. 'And I never wanted to love you. I am...' He hesitated. 'OK, I'll admit it, I'm a total romantic.'

'Anyone who has the dreams you had and makes them come true must be a romantic,' she said, trembling at the passion on his strained face.

'I have always idealised women, finding them sadly lacking. When we first met, I was dazzled, bemused, aroused and intrigued. I wanted to know you better. And I knew I must love you when I cared what happened to you. The thought of other men touching you made me want to kill them!' He sighed. 'I was in serious trouble. Sentiment filled my head. I had dreams. Us on our wedding-day, at our children's christenings, growing old with you——'

'Vigadó!' she whispered shakily. 'We can make those dreams come true. If we love each other, we can't possibly hurt one another. We both like our independence. We're both strong, we have careers to pursue——'

'I—I would find it hard to live anywhere but Hungary,' he said huskily. 'But if that's what you want, we'll find somewhere near your father.'

She thought of his youthful dream: how he'd stood by the Danube and sworn to be living on Castle Hill one day. She thought of the look in his eyes and the shake in his voice when they'd viewed the crown of St Stephen. And she knew without a shadow of doubt that he must love her very much to consider living anywhere other than Hungary.

'No.' She smiled shakily. 'I want to see Father often, but I could be happy here—and you would mourn for Hungary. You have too much to do, a lot of your dream to fulfil here. You will make your peace with Eva and you will need to be near Lindi. It's not what I want.'

He helped her to her feet and for a moment they clung together, the tears trickling down Mariann's cheeks. 'What's the matter, my darling?' he finally asked in fond concern.

'I'm so ha-a-ppy!' She sniffed. At his chuckle, she bent and quickly grabbed a handful of snow, pushing it directly in his face. 'Don't you laugh at me!' she yelled, squealing and darting away as he quickly formed a snowball and hurled it at her back. She was rugby-tackled to the ground. 'This is not romantic,' she said indignantly to the laughing Vigadó.

'Watch this space,' he murmured. And for the next hour he proved that it was romantic. So was the warm bath they had together, the champagne they drank by the roaring log fire afterwards, the chocolates he fed her, one by one, kiss by kiss. And then came the long, romantic night.

Waking at dawn the next morning in the huge four-poster bed, she thought how happy she was and hugged herself, thinking of the foursomes they'd have with Tanya and István, of the long telephone conversations she'd have with her father and with Sue. She stretched luxuriously.

'I love you,' murmured a sleepy Vigadó. 'So much! I want to put the world in your hands.'

'I'd rather have a cheese and pickle sandwich,' she said hopefully.

He laughed in delight, hugging her, and then touched his lips to hers. 'Do we like our obsession?' he asked huskily.

'We do,' she whispered passionately. And she knew what she'd refused to admit before: that she needn't run from love any longer because Vigadó had unchained her heart. 'I think I fell in love with you when I first saw your photograph, even before we met. Instant bondage!' she husked.

Vigadó kissed her tenderly. 'Let me bind you a little more,' he said softly. 'I intend to make you earn that cheese and pickle!' He drew her to him, capturing her mouth, possessing her with a profoundly tender sweetness.

A little later they made that foursome with István and Tanya. And when she saw the loving looks between her sister and István, Mariann knew that they were only mirroring the tender admiration that shone in her eyes and in Vigadó's.

'Only Sue to go,' laughed Tanya softly, her face glowing with happiness.

'Not her,' sighed Mariann. 'She's far too blinkered.'

'Love has a way of removing blinkers,' said Vigadó huskily, stroking Mariann's hair. 'To our destinies,' he murmured, raising his glass.

Mariann smiled blissfully at him. 'Our destinies,' she said softly. 'May we always be as happy as we are at this moment.'

* * * * *

If you enjoyed this book, we hope you'll watch out next month for the final part of this trilogy, THREADS OF DESTINY, in which we meet the youngest Evans sister, Suzanne— and her gorgeous, mysterious hero László!

HARLEQUIN PRESENTS®

Don't be late for the wedding!

Be sure to make a date in your diary for the happy event—
the latest in our tantalizing new selection of stories...

Bonded in matrimony, torn by desire...

Coming next month:

THE ULTIMATE BETRAYAL by Michelle Reid
Harlequin Presents #1799

"...an explosive magic that only (Michelle) Reid can create."
—*Affaire de Coeur*

The perfect marriage...the perfect family? That's what
Rachel Masterton had always believed she and her husband
Daniel shared. Then Rachel was told that Daniel had betrayed
her and she realized that she had to fight to save her marriage.
But she also had to fight to forgive Daniel for this...the
ultimate betrayal.

Available in March wherever Harlequin books are sold.

HARLEQUIN PRESENTS®

Ever felt the excitement of a dangerous desire...?

The thrill of a feverish flirtation...?

Passion is guaranteed with the latest in our new
selection of sensual stories.

Indulge in...

Dangerous Liaisons

Falling in love is a risky affair

Coming next month:

Dark Victory by ELIZABETH OLDFIELD
Harlequin Presents #1800

Five years ago Cheska had given Lawson her heart *and* her
body *and* her soul.

So he'd loved her...and then he'd left her!

Now he was back—wanting to pick up the pieces.

Cheska might not be the same trusting and naive girl
Lawson had once known...but he seemed willing to
love the woman she'd become.

Available in March wherever Harlequin books are sold.